"You loved mein love with y

"And now?" she asked quietly, wondering how he could love the sort of person she had become if she was so different from before.

"I love you more than ever. Actually it's like loving a different woman, and you are wonderful."

Karina closed her eyes as a tremor ran through her and she felt herself being pulled insistently against him to feel once again the heat of him, the masculine hardness, the desire which he had kept under control for so very, very long.

Born in the industrial heart of England, **MARGARET MAYO** now lives in a Staffordshire countryside village. She became a writer by accident, after attempting to write a short story when she was almost forty, and now writing is one of the most enjoyable parts of her life. She combines her hobby of photography with her research.

FORGOTTEN ENGAGEMENT

MARGARET MAYO

AN ENGAGEMENT OF CONVENIENCE

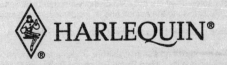

TORONTO • NEW YORK • LONDON
AMSTERDAM • PARIS • SYDNEY • HAMBURG
STOCKHOLM • ATHENS • TOKYO • MILAN • MADRID
PRAGUE • WARSAW • BUDAPEST • AUCKLAND

ISBN 0-373-80635-3

FORGOTTEN ENGAGEMENT

First North American Publication 2000.

Copyright © 1998 by Margaret Mayo.

www.eHarlequin.com

Printed in U.S.A.

CHAPTER ONE

'KARINA, you've been crying.'

Karina cursed silently because she had hoped Ford wouldn't notice. He knew her too well—that was the trouble. 'I'm a bit down today,' she admitted quietly, not bothering to get up from her armchair as he entered the room. He was a tall, good-looking man in his mid-thirties, black-haired, like herself, and with dark eyes, a sensual mouth and a nose that was almost too long but not quite. 'Do we have to go out?'

'I think we should. You stay in too much.' He stooped to drop a kiss on her forehead, his fingers lightly brushing her cheek. Nothing else, just that, but Karina felt the tension in him, the urge to do much more—perhaps to gather her in his arms and rain kisses on her face. She couldn't help but admire his self-control.

She wondered sometimes why she didn't love him, why she hadn't fallen for this totally gorgeous man who'd taken over her life. She'd never found an answer.

Ford seated himself in the car opposite, his long legs outstretched, his dark eyes watchful. 'Care to tell me about it?'

'About what?' She smiled, the carefree smile she adopted for his benefit, the one which hid the heartache and despair. With her face devoid of makeup, wearing a simple white cotton dress and with her long black hair in a plait, Karina looked little more than half her twenty-six years.

'Why you're down in the dumps.'

She lifted her narrow shoulders and let them drop again in an unconsciously elegant gesture. 'I'm better now you're here.' Immediately she knew that had been the wrong thing to say. He would surely put the wrong interpretation on it. And he did.

A smile widened his already generous lips. 'If it's because you're missing me then perhaps I ought to become a more permanent part of your life.'

Wishing she could retract her words, Karina shrank into the corner of her chair, her arms folded across her chest in a defensive gesture, her cobalt blue eyes wide and apprehensive.

She had known this was coming and ought to have been prepared, yet she wasn't. The thought of becoming something more to Ford frightened her half to death. She owed it to him, and yet she couldn't face the thought of committing herself totally to a man she didn't love.

Dark eyes narrowed in the tanned hard face, and to her surprise he looked annoyed by her reaction. This man who'd been as gentle as a kitten with her for over twelve months was suddenly different. 'I'm sorry the idea scares you, Karina, but I think I've been patient long enough. I think the time has come for us to have a serious talk.'

There was an edge to his tone, a sternness that she'd never heard before. Karina shivered.

'I need to know,' he said, 'exactly what your feelings for me are.'

'You…you know what they are,' she answered quietly, huskily, rubbing the goose-bumps that had risen on her arms. Outside the sun was blazing, yet Karina felt as if an Arctic blast had hit her.

'You've never put them into words,' he reminded her, his eyes intent on her face. 'I know you see me as someone to depend on, someone who has helped you through the bad times, but—and you must know this—I want more. Much more, Karina. You loved me once. I need to know whether you can love me again.'

But how did she know that she'd once loved him? Since the accident Karina could remember nothing—not who she was or where she came from. She was living in a void and sometimes the burden of it was more than she could bear.

Ford Fielding claimed to be her boyfriend but she had no recollection of him. Her memory had been completely wiped out. She'd even had to learn to talk again, as well as to talk, to read, to write—to do the thousand and one things everyone else took for granted—and Ford had been with her every inch of the way, encouraging, persuading, praising, showing remarkable patience and understanding.

He'd told her that both her parents were dead, that she had no siblings and that she'd been brought up by foster-parents until she'd been old enough to fend for herself. So all she had was Ford, whether she liked it or not.

It was a difficult situation. She didn't want to hurt his feelings. He'd been so good to her, so kind, so caring, so compassionate. How could she insult him by declaring that she felt nothing. 'I don't know for sure that I once loved you,' she said brokenly. 'I only have your word for that. You're rushing me, Ford.'

'Rushing you?' he said fiercely. 'That's the under-statement of the century. I personally think I've been very patient.'

He had, oh, yes, he had. For several months after she'd come out of hospital he'd lived with her in this luxurious Thames-side apartment for which he paid the rent. He'd tended to her every need, done everything—

except sleep with her. A lesser man would have given up long ago, but not Ford. He'd put his own job on hold to help her—she would never have managed without him. But as for loving him, it had simply never happened.

He was someone to lean on, depend on, but not to go to bed with. It was odd, really, that she felt nothing for him because Ford Fielding was every woman's dream, powerfully built, handsome and wealthy, and he had confessed that it was time he got married. He could have had his pick of any number of women and yet he'd stayed with her.

'You've been patient,' she agreed. 'More than I expected or deserved. I wouldn't have blamed you if you'd turned your back on me.'

Ford nodded slowly. 'Maybe I should have done. Maybe I've done you no favours.'

'I won't hold it against you if you walk out now.' Possibly her love would return, given time. On the other hand, it might not. There was no way of knowing. She rested her head on the palm of one hand. She didn't want this problem. She didn't want to have to think about it. Maybe it would be best if Ford *did* wash his hands of her.

'Karina?' He was waiting for her to say more.

She looked at him and grimaced. 'I know what you want to hear, Ford, but I can't. I find it impossible to…to feel any love for you…in the way you want. I love you, of course I do, but only as a friend. I think the time has come for me to move out. I'll get a job, find somewhere I can afford, and—'

'That's out of the question, Karina,' he said sharply. 'You're not ready for that yet. Nor is it what I want, and you know it.'

'But if I—'

'Dammit, Karina, you don't know what you're talking about. I don't think you even know what it is that I expect of you.'

'Yes, I do,' she whispered painfully. She didn't want to hear it.

He got up and walked over to her. He held out his hands and she was given no choice but to put hers into them and let him pull her to her feet. Then he took her into his arms and held her slender, trembling body close to his.

He had held her before but this was different. This was not comfort for the sick and wounded—this was a man holding a woman, a man full of desire, a man no longer in control of his feelings.

Karina felt tears squeeze out of her eyes. He was going to be so disappointed.

If only they hadn't argued, thought Ford. If he hadn't accused Karina of two-timing him, she wouldn't have thrown her engagement ring in his face and stormed out of the house. She wouldn't have had the accident. She wouldn't have lost her memory. They would have been married by now, possibly even started a family. Everything had been his fault. He would never be able to forgive himself—never.

More times than he could count Ford had regretted that day, regretted every single second of it. The argument was as clear in his mind as if it had happened only yesterday instead of over twelve months ago.

He should have listened to Karina. He should have trusted her, instead of flinging accusations left, right and centre and giving her no chance to put her side of the story.

'You were seen with another man,' he'd raged. 'And not only on one occasion. With a lord, no less. Is it the peerage you're interested in? Am I not good enough for you?'

'You're making a mistake, Ford. I—'

'No, you're the one who's making the mistake, Karina. If you think that—'

'Ford, please listen to me. I love you, and I would never—'

'Why should I listen when you don't give a damn about my feelings?' He hadn't wanted her excuses. 'What do you think—that I'll forgive and forget if you promise not to see him again? I'm not that stupid. I know what it would be like in another few months' time. You'd—'

'Ford, please listen.'

'No, you listen to me, Karina. I know exactly—'

'But you don't. Please let me—'

'Shut up, Karina. I refuse to listen to your excuses. I know perfectly well that—'

'Damn you, Stafford Fielding, you know nothing,' she had cried, her face suffused with anger. 'If you won't listen, if you can't trust me, then you can have your rotten ring back and do what the hell you like with it.' With shaking fingers she'd wrested it off her finger and thrown it furiously at him. 'I hope you're satisfied now. This is the end, I can promise you that. You'll never see me again.' With her head high, her back ramrod straight, she'd marched out of the room.

He'd made no attempt to stop her but how many times since then he'd wished that he had. How many times. If only he'd gone after her she would never have been knocked down. If only he'd listened to her side of the story. If, if, if…

No lord had come to visit her in the hospital. No one, except himself. It had been a sad state of affairs.

Having been told that he must wait for her memory to return naturally, not to try and force it, he'd said nothing to Karina about their engagement, about the fantastic love life they'd had—or the ending of it. And certainly nothing about her infidelity. Karina herself had never asked any intimate questions, almost as though she was deliberately steering clear of personal issues.

He'd realised, very early on, that he still loved her, and that her fling with Charles Forester had made not a jot of difference. He also took all the blame for her accident. It kept him awake night after night, and the fact that she seemed to love him no longer was torture of the worst kind.

Ford was sure her memory loss was only temporary, even though the neurosurgeon had told him that with brain injuries of this kind occasionally, rarely, a person's memory never came back. He'd promised himself he would be patient but he was slowly reaching the end of his endurance.

The feel of her slender, quivering body against him, the scent of her perfumed skin in his nostrils, was almost his undoing. How many times in the last twelve months had he wanted to hold her like this, to stroke her gloriously thick shining hair, to touch his lips to her ivory skin, to taste her, to take, to recreate the old magic, to make her his, to become one, to…?

He heard the groan in the back of his throat but didn't associate it with himself. Without conscious thought his arms tightened around her and his mouth bent to hers.

With his eyes closed he drank the honey-sweet nectar he'd been denied for so long, and for a second he thought she wasn't going to resist—for a second his heart rioted and every male hormone ran amok.

He prepared to advance his onslaught, but Karina flung back her head and cried out in anguish, 'No! No! I don't want this.'

Ford knew he should heed her words but need took over, need and hunger and desire—pent up too long, grown too strong—and once he'd started he couldn't stop.

'Karina,' he murmured, one hand coming behind her head to gently guide her mouth back to his, 'please don't fight me, please don't be afraid. I promise not to make you do anything you don't want to do, but you need to kiss me to find out what your true feelings are.'

'I know that I don't love you, Ford,' she retorted. 'A kiss will make no difference.'

He could hear the pain in her voice but it was nothing compared to the hurt she was inflicting on him. It felt as though she had pierced his heart with a knife and, not content with that, was turning it slowly, excruciatingly slowly.

He had to do something quickly before the pain became unbearable. His mouth claimed hers again but it took every ounce of his not inconsiderable will-power not to deepen the kiss, not to drink hungrily from her lips.

It was a tender kiss, an exploratory kiss. There was nothing in it that could frighten her, nothing to make her want to tear herself away from him.

He felt no response, however, only the tremors that still racked her slender body. Gradually, seemingly a lifetime later, she grew still, and although she did not entirely relax in his arms she was no longer fighting him.

Her lips never took nor gave. They remained passive

beneath his, inert, telling him nothing. He touched them with a thousand tiny kisses, traced their outline with the tip of his tongue, lightly stroked her chin with a gentle thumb. He touched her ears, her eyes. Everything he did was designed to stir emotions long since dead.

Just when despair took over, when he was prepared to give up—to move out of her life if that was what she wanted—he felt the flicker of a response. He felt her lips tremble beneath his, he felt it reverberate through her entire body—and this time it was not fear!

Nevertheless, he remained cautious and kept his kisses as light as the brush of a butterfly's wing, still tantalising her. One wrong step now and he would lose his faint advantage.

When she went limp against him, when her lips opened of their own free will, he knew that round one was to him. He held back for a moment, looking into her softly blushing face. Her eyes were closed, as though she wanted to deny any feelings that he'd managed to arouse in her.

He kissed her again, deepening it this time, hesitantly exploring the soft inner moistness of her mouth. Lord, she had never tasted so good. He wanted more, and he wanted it now, but he must still be cautious.

When her tongue entwined with his and her lips responded with the beginnings of a very real passion it felt as though a thousand stars had exploded inside his head.

He cupped her face with both hands and pulled down her lower lip with his thumb, kissing and tasting and indulging himself in the sheer heady pleasure of once again kissing the woman he had thought lost to him for ever.

'Karina, look at me.' He wanted to see her eyes

stormy with desire, he wanted to know that this was for real—not a figment of his imagination.

Slowly—reluctantly, it seemed to him—she dragged her eyelids open, and Ford drew in a rapid breath when he saw the deep blue of her eyes. They only ever went this dark when she was fully aroused.

'Oh, Karina,' he breathed harshly, but when he attempted to kiss her again she backed away.

'I think we should stop here,' she said faintly. 'I don't know what is happening to me. I'm not sure that I can cope with it.'

'What's happening is that you're becoming alive again,' he told her, smiling warmly. 'I was beginning to think it might never happen.'

'How can I feel like this when I don't love you?' she asked, looking and sounding like a little girl lost.

'I think you do love me, but your mind won't let you admit it,' he told her.

'How long had we known each other before my accident?'

'Thirteen months.' He'd told her this before but she must have forgotten. She'd had lots of memory lapses in the first few months—silly things, like putting potatoes on to boil and then forgetting all about them—but gradually her memory had improved until she was almost back to normal.

She gave a twisted smile. 'Unlucky thirteen. Could I drive?'

Ford inclined his head, wondering at her deft change of subject.

'So, will you teach me to drive again?'

'If it's what you want.' He resigned himself to the fact that their kissing was over, but at least it had been a start. He'd proved that she wasn't entirely immune to him. 'If you think you're ready for it.'

'I'm ready,' she agreed eagerly. 'Let's begin now, shall we?'

'But we're going to Paul and Marie's for lunch,' he reminded her.

A shadow crossed her face. 'Can't you ring and tell them something's cropped up?'

He nodded, unable to dash her enthusiasm. 'I guess I can.'

But in the end it was his own bubble that burst, his heart that dropped with despair into the very pit of his stomach. They were in the car and he was explaining the gears when Karina suddenly turned her big blue eyes on him and said, 'Who is Lord Forester?'

CHAPTER TWO

'LORD FORESTER?' Ford's face was grave as he looked at Karina, his heartbeat erratic and painful. If she was remembering, and Charles Forester's name was the first that came to mind, it surely spelled disaster.

'Yes.' Karina nodded, her blue eyes narrowed in a frown of concentration. 'The name just jumped into my mind. I wondered whether it was someone I knew.'

He wanted to say that he'd never heard the name but his conscience wouldn't let him. 'I believe you did know him, but it's not someone I've met myself. I can't tell you anything about him.' And even if he could he wouldn't. He needed time to win back Karina's love before she remembered the truth behind their parting, before she remembered Charles Forester clearly and what he had meant to her.

'At least it's a start,' she said. 'It's the first signal I've had that my memory is coming back.' She smiled happily at him. 'It's quite exciting, isn't it?'

Ford wondered if she noticed that he didn't share her enthusiasm.

The first driving lesson went without a hitch. Karina proved to be an instinctive driver, and she was feeling extremely pleased with herself when she pulled up outside the block of luxurious apartments, so much so that when they got out of the car she threw her arms around Ford and kissed his cheek. 'That was wonderful, thank you. When can we go again?'

He smiled down into her animated face. 'Tomorrow?'

She nodded blissfully, unaware that Ford's arm was still around her as they made their way inside. 'It's as though I've been driving for ever. It's a quite marvellous feeling.'

It wasn't until they were in the lift that Ford turned her in his arms and kissed her, and because Karina was in such high spirits she kissed him back, without even thinking about it.

His earlier kiss had taken her by surprise. She'd been prepared to hate it, to fight him off, but his gentle persistence had triggered an unexpected response. She'd found to her amazement that his kiss had not been unpleasant, that, in fact, she'd quite liked it.

And she was enjoying this kiss, too!

There were no thoughts now of pushing him away and she sensed that Ford, too, was a little shocked because he pulled back for a brief space to look enquiringly into her eyes.

'It's all right,' she whispered shyly.

With no more encouragement his arms tightened and his kiss deepened, and Karina found herself enjoying the feel of his hard body against hers—thighs against thighs, chest against chest, hearts pounding, heat flooding, desire building.

For over twelve months she'd felt numb. She'd seen Ford only as a friend, and at times he'd irritated her with his constant presence. Now she realised how hard it must have been for him. He'd stood by her side through it all—through her illness, her rehabilitation, her black moods, her forgetfulness. He'd always been there for her and he'd given no inkling that inside he was burning with fierce desire.

Karina also knew that she must be careful. If she gave

him too much encouragement he might think that she was prepared to take up where they had left off—and that wasn't what she wanted. She wanted to remember her past before she got on with her future.

When the lift came to a halt she pulled away from him and walked into the apartment. The spacious lounge had a sumptuous ivory carpet and pale yellow walls with pen and ink drawings of cartoon characters. Its shelves and tables held an impressive array of porcelain clowns, juggling coloured balls, riding unicycles or simply being clowns. When he would have taken her into his arms again Karina shook her head. 'You're going too quickly for me, Ford.'

To her surprise his thick brows rose in disbelief. 'I've had the patience of a saint this last twelve months. You certainly can't accuse me of rushing you.'

'You know what I mean,' she said, and in an attempt to avoid him she slid open the glass doors and stepped out onto the balcony.

On the River Thames below a young man who was teaching his girlfriend to row caught her attention, especially when she lost one of the oars and fell in a heap in the boat, laughing. Her boyfriend pulled her up and kissed her and they were oblivious to the fact that a cruiser was fast bearing down on them.

Karina missed what happened next because Ford joined her and turned her to face him. The desire had gone from his face, replaced by a grim mouth and hard, penetrating eyes. 'Am I wasting my time, Karina?'

She frowned. 'What do you mean?'

'I think you know but, if you wish, I will spell it out.'

Karina shivered, despite the warmth of the day. Ford in this mood scared her. He was her mainstay, her sole contact with the outside world.

'You must know, Karina, that the reason I've hung around all this time is because I thought that one day we would get back on the same footing as before.'

'Which was?' She had always fought shy of asking him exactly how far their relationship had gone.

'You were my fiancée. We were planning to get married.'

Karina felt the air rush from her lungs. 'I didn't realise,' she said breathlessly. 'Why didn't you tell me? Is this what you've been waiting for? You want me to— to marry you?' She owed it to Ford, she supposed, but how could she marry a man she didn't love? Surely he didn't expect her to go through with it under the circumstances? It was only now, twelve long months after the accident, that they had kissed. It was far too soon to enter into anything deeper or more permanent.

'It was in my mind,' he answered.

Karina frowned. 'If we were engaged, why wasn't I wearing your ring?' She looked down at her hand, as if trying to imagine one there. It would be something large and expensive, she supposed. He would have spared no expense.

His reply was a long time in coming. She saw the mixture of emotions crossing his face, his reluctance to answer. 'We'd had an argument,' he admitted eventually. 'You threw it back at me.'

Karina frowned, unable to imagine herself being so impulsive. 'What did we argue about?'

Again his answer took ages. 'I'm afraid I accused you of seeing someone else behind my back.'

A further shock wave ran through her. Surely not. It didn't feel right. She wouldn't two-time him. It wasn't in her nature. 'Did I admit it?' she asked tentatively.

Ford shook his head. 'That's the trouble—I didn't

give you a chance to put your side of the story. And my refusal to listen made you so angry that you threw the ring at me and walked out. That was the day you had the accident.'

'I see,' she said quietly as she tried to take in this sudden and unexpected information. 'I wondered why I hadn't been more alert, why I had allowed someone to snatch my bag.'

'Even so, you shouldn't have chased after him,' Ford said sternly, 'because then you'd never have been knocked down, none of this would have happened, I wouldn't be feeling so—'

'The thing is,' interrupted Karina, 'I can't believe I would be unfaithful to you.'

Ford drew in a long uneven breath. 'That's as may be, but the accident was definitely my fault. You told me when you walked out of the door that I would never see you again. And when Geoffrey phoned and told me that you'd been hit by a car and taken into hospital I thought you'd thrown yourself under it deliberately. I thought you'd tried to end your life. I can't tell you what pain I felt.'

He bowed his head, his jaw muscles in spasm and his fingers twisting in anguish. 'And when you were in a coma for almost two weeks I nearly went out of my mind. I shall never forgive myself, ever. If I hadn't been such a bastard, if I'd listened to what you'd had to say, you'd never have had that accident.'

'You would have forgiven my little indiscretion—if I did have one?' Karina still found it difficult to accept that she would have done such a thing. Twelve months wasn't long to know herself, but she was sure she wasn't the type to indulge in affairs behind her fiancé's back.

Ford nodded. 'I know now that I love you too much

to let you go. I think I love you more than I did before.'
He looked at her then, his dark eyes shadowed, determination tightening his jaw. 'And I think you could learn
to love me again—given time. Meanwhile…' There was
a slight pause. 'I don't think you'd find marriage to me
such a hardship.'

Karina had begun to feel sorry for him, had begun to
realise what a burden he carried, but now she said angrily, 'You're saying this because it's what *you* want,
aren't you? You're still not considering me. Have you
any idea what I've gone through? What's still in front
of me? My whole life is a mystery. My memory may
never come back. How can I marry a man who says I
love him when I don't know if it's the truth? Surely if
I loved you before I would love you now?'

He nodded slowly, sadly. 'It would seem logical.'

'So you can see my dilemma?'

'I think, Karina,' he said with ill-concealed impatience, 'that you're overlooking the obvious—that I
know you better than you know yourself.'

She drew in an angry breath. She most certainly
wasn't going to let Ford bulldoze her into something she
wasn't ready for, no matter how much sense he made.
'Maybe you do at this moment. But it won't always be
like this. There'll be a time when I remember everything—who I am, what my feelings for you are, everything. Lord, I could marry you and then find out that
you're my worst enemy.'

Turning to look over the balcony again, Karina saw
that the cruiser had miraculously missed the rowing boat
and somehow the lovers had retrieved the lost oar and
were heading towards the opposite bank, their troubles
over. She wished hers could be solved so easily.

Ford said, 'I'm sorry you feel that way.'

He didn't sound apologetic—in fact, he sounded extremely cross—and Karina couldn't understand his attitude. For months they'd had a warm and compassionate relationship. He'd been patient and kind and had put her before himself every time, but now he was spoiling things by wanting more from her than she was prepared to give.

'I'm sorry *you* feel as you do,' she said, still with her back to him, watching the boats on the river. 'If that's all you've been waiting for maybe it's time we called it a day.'

'*Hell, no!*' He spoke so loudly that Karina jumped. 'That's not what I want at all.'

'But I don't want you harassing me.' She spoke primly, her back straight, her eyes looking straight ahead but seeing nothing now except the torment of her own soul. Ford was putting pressure on her that she couldn't handle, wasn't ready for. She'd discovered a new side to his character today. What else was in store?

'I wasn't aware of doing that,' he said fiercely. 'A couple of kisses hardly constitutes harassment, Karina. If you're honest with yourself you'll admit that you didn't find them offensive. In fact, quite the opposite.'

'So?' She swung around, her eyes blazing in her heated face. 'A kiss doesn't constitute an agreement of marriage.'

'You're suggesting that we forget I said anything?'

'Yes.'

'For how long?'

'For as long as it takes.'

He snorted angrily. 'Hell, Karina, I'm not made of stone.'

She compressed her lips into a thin straight line. 'In that case, you'd better find yourself another girlfriend.'

Even as she said the words Karina knew that she didn't mean them, but neither was she ready to enter into a sexual relationship with Ford.

'There are times, Karina, when I could swear you're a different girl.' Ford shook his head as he spoke, looking at her through narrowed, speculative eyes.

'Maybe I am different. No one survives such a serious accident and comes out of it exactly the same. If you don't like what you see then—'

'Don't start that again,' he cut in harshly.

'Start what?' she asked, her own anger showing. 'If you ask me, you're the one with the problem. I think you should go home. In fact, I think we shouldn't see each other for a few days so that you can think things over.'

'I don't need to think things over,' he growled. 'I know what I want.'

'Except that it's not the same as I want,' Karina declared, 'and I refuse to be rushed.' She walked back inside and picked up one of the porcelain clowns. His cheerful, ridiculous face did not make her smile.

'How long do you think I shall have to wait?'

Her lovely blue eyes widened as she looked at him. 'How on earth am I supposed to know that?'

'A month? A year? Forever?'

'Wave a magic wand, why don't you?' she snapped. 'This is a pointless conversation, Ford, and you know it. If you cannot accept things the way they are, don't bother to come round here again. It's as simple as that.'

'Is that what you want?' Eyes as dark and as cold as a stormy winter's night looked into hers. They made Karina shiver. It was not what she wanted but it might be for the best. They were getting nowhere, talking like this.

It was unbelievable that a couple of kisses had started them fighting, the first time since her accident that they'd had any cross words. He'd been a man of amazing tolerance and endless patience, yet he was now champing at the bit to take her to bed and to marry her—to make her his for the rest of their lives.

Maybe if he'd been patient a little longer it would have happened naturally. Now he'd spoilt it; he'd marred their friendship. It would never get back on the same footing.

Ford drew his car to a halt in front of his Hampstead house, berating himself for being so stupid. It was inconceivable that he'd done such a thing. Talk about being irrational. What the hell had happened to him?

A kiss was what had happened. It had unlocked a gamut of emotions which he had kept on a tight rein for what had seemed a lifetime. Another man would have sought relief elsewhere but, no, he hadn't done that. He had convinced himself he could wait.

And now he'd ruined everything!

Karina had all but thrown him out. In fact, it he hadn't left when he had, she probably would have done. He'd never seen her so angry before—and never with him, only ever with herself.

He marched straight into his study, where he kept a decanter of whisky, and poured himself a generous measure. Dammit! Damn, damn, damn. What had come over him? Why hadn't he controlled his urges? Why hadn't he kept his mouth shut?

He swallowed the whisky in one go and poured another. He paced the room and continued to castigate himself. What he'd done had been beyond reproach until he'd kissed her. He could understand Karina's anger even though he couldn't understand her reaction. He was absolutely certain that she'd found his kisses enjoyable—more than that, they had aroused feelings in her which for some reason she wanted to deny. Why? What was she afraid of?

It had hurt when she'd said that she didn't love him. He had thought—he had hoped—that when they kissed it would trigger memories of how she'd once felt—except, of course, that it could also remind her that she'd indulged in an affair with Charles Forester!

He'd been afraid she might remember more about Charles when he'd told her about their broken engagement, and had been enormously relieved when she hadn't. His plan of action now had to be to make her fall in love with him again before she did remember. He had to start anew—woo her, persuade her, convince her. The very thought of it set his pulses racing. It was a challenge, an exciting one—and one that he intended to win.

If her memory did come back—no, *when* it came back—then he wanted her to be so much in love with him—preferably married to him—that she wouldn't give her former lover another thought.

He had to be careful, though. He had to handle her with kid gloves. He would give her the few days that she wanted and then he would start his campaign. He would send her flowers, he would ask her for a date and he wouldn't even kiss her on their first few times out. And he would no longer let himself into her apartment, but would respect her privacy.

His plan of action decided upon, Ford felt much better and finally sat down. He had a pile of work on his desk which needed attention and he was soon completely immersed in it. Although he had left the running of his

computer business in Geoffrey's very capable hands—
Geoffrey being his sales director and also his best
friend—it was perhaps time that he took up the reins
again.

The next few days were the hardest of his life. So
many times he wanted to pick up the phone and call
Karina; so many times he wanted to go and see her—
not only because he was anxious to put his plan into
action but because he needed to know whether she was
all right, whether she was coping, whether she had any
problems. He had always been there for her.

There had been many difficulties in the beginning
when her relearning process had begun. Ford had taught
her to read, to write, to cook—they'd had lots of fun
then. He'd taught her to do a hundred and one things
which had once been second nature to her. Something
as simple as tying shoelaces, for instance.

And still, after all these months, there were times
when she needed to ask him for advice. Would she be
too proud now? Would she ask someone else? The
thought didn't please him and he picked up the phone—
only to replace it. Then he picked it up again and dialled
the florist's. It was time to start his campaign.

Yellow roses—her favourite. She'd been ordering
flowers the first time he had met her. He had been rushing into the florist's as she'd been coming out, and he'd
almost knocked her over.

As his arms had come out to steady her he had caught
the delicate scent of her perfume, had felt the slender
softness of her body, the velvety texture of her skin, and
had known that this was a woman he wanted to see
again—tall, leggy, with long shining black hair and the
most enchanting blue eyes he had ever seen.

He had persuaded the shop assistant to give him her

address and had immediately ordered a huge bouquet of yellow roses to be sent to her, with a note apologising once again for cannoning into her.

The next evening he had turned up on her doorstep. She had looked at him, stunned. 'You! What are you doing here? The flowers were apology enough, and far more than was warranted. How did you know they were my favourite?'

'A lucky guess,' he admitted. 'Aren't you going to ask me in? If you have no plans for this evening I thought we could share this...' he produced a bottle of Dom Perignon from behind his back '...and tell each other our life stories.'

Her red angora sweater emphasised the enchanting shape of her breasts and Ford felt an insane urge to stroke them. He wanted to hold her, to kiss her, to— He slapped the thoughts down immediately. That was madness.

Karina looked at the champagne and then at Ford. 'This is highly irregular. I don't even know your name.'

'Stafford Fielding,' he said at once. 'Ford to my friends.'

'But you're not a friend—you're a stranger. I was always taught to beware of strangers.'

'And how can we reconcile that if we don't talk?' he asked innocently.

She smiled, her stunning blue eyes sparkling. 'Very well, Stafford Fielding,' she said, 'you may come in for a few minutes, but the truth is that I do have other plans.'

'A boyfriend?' He felt a rush of disappointment. This was the girl of his dreams—he couldn't bear the thought that she was committed to someone else.

She shook her head and smiled as she stood back and

allowed him to enter.

'I'm going to the cinema with a girlfriend.'

'Then ring and cancel,' he said at once, relief washing over him. 'I'm sure she won't mind.'

'Not if I tell her the guy who sent the beautiful roses has turned up on my doorstep,' she said with a laugh. 'She couldn't get over it. No man has ever sent her flowers, and the fact that they were from a total stranger made it all the more intriguing as far as she was concerned.'

'Maybe I should send her some as well,' said Ford, looking pleased. 'Especially if she relinquishes you to me for the evening.'

Karina laughed again as she led the way into her tiny sitting room. He thought it the most wonderful sound he'd ever heard, but at the same time he wondered how she managed to live in such cramped conditions. His bathroom alone was larger than this room. It was clean and tidy, but everything was worn, and if it hadn't been for his flowers, spilling everywhere, it would have been cheerless.

'Rented?' he asked his eyebrows raised.

Karina nodded. 'I'm sorry it's not much, but it's all I can afford at the moment.'

He nodded. 'I'm not criticising—it reminds me of one I once rented.' He made a mental note to get her out of it as soon as he could. It never occurred to him that she wouldn't want to date him. No girl ever turned him down.

By the end of the evening he felt as though he had known her all his life, and a few weeks later he moved Karina into an apartment he had found for her on the bank of the Thames.

She was totally overwhelmed.

He had wanted her to move into his Georgian house in Hampstead, but she'd refused—said she didn't know him well enough. She accepted the apartment, however, and he actually spent more time with her there than he did at home. Their sex life was incredible. He had never met a girl who enjoyed it as much as Karina did.

It was what made her attitude now all the more difficult to understand. A memory loss, yes, but actual physical feelings? He was not so sure—and he was half inclined to believe that it was Charles who'd taken that part of her away from him.

Jealousy seared him like a red hot poker, and he was fiercely determined to win her back before she was lost to him for ever. Her memory could return any day—and then it would be goodbye to him and hello again to Charles Forester.

The days were long without Ford. Karina tried to keep herself busy but there was only so much she could do— so much furniture to polish, so many rooms to vacuum, so many windows to clean. And they didn't need doing every day.

Most of her neighbours worked and, although they had called in to see her when she'd first come out of hospital, once they'd discovered that Ford was in twenty-four-hour attendance they didn't bother her again.

She was unhappy with her own company. She had grown used to Ford over the last months and it felt strange without him. She'd thought she'd wanted her independence but now she felt isolated. He didn't even ring.

Feeling that the time had come to do something about her future, Karina enquired about college courses in graphic design—Ford had told her that this was what she used to do—but the classes didn't start until September. So she still had several weeks of doing nothing. She had never felt so alone.

One night she had a dream. She dreamt that she was being made love to, long slow hours of exquisite, erotic love-making, the most incredible sensations filling her body.

It was not until she awoke and began to think about her dream that she realised it hadn't been Ford who had been making love to her but a good-looking, fair-haired man named Charles.

Who was Charles? Was he someone from her past? Someone she knew? Or just a dream figure, no one in particular? Whoever he was, he'd certainly brought her body alive with effortless ease. She could still feel a buzz through her veins, and still felt an urge to lift her body to accommodate him. It was madness.

A cool shower helped, but not much. The dream had seemed very real, and the trouble now was that she kept putting Ford in place of the man named Charles—imagined he was the one who had made such perfect love to her, imagined herself back in his arms, felt his love flow into her, felt her body come vibrantly alive again—despite the fact that she'd made it very clear to him that she wasn't interested in a physical relationship.

Had she been wrong? Was this what she wanted? Did she love Ford, even though she kept denying it?

Around mid-morning, just as Karina was thinking about going for a walk—anywhere to drive the torment from her mind—a huge bouquet of yellow roses arrived. There was no card, nothing to say who had sent them, but she knew they were from Ford because who else would send her flowers?

And yet, if he knew her as well as he professed, then he would know that she disliked yellow roses. She didn't very much like roses at all, but especially not yellow ones. She had no idea why—she just knew it.

It was all very strange, she thought as she arranged them in a vase and stood them on the hall table. She could have put them in her sitting room where they would have matched the decor—perhaps that's what Ford had had in mind—but she couldn't stand the thought of looking at them all day long.

Although she knew she ought to ring and thank him, Karina decided to go out on her walk first. The sky was blue, with only the occasional white cloud, the sun warm, and everyone was cheerful and smiling. She felt sightly better.

She caught a bus into Richmond and looked around the shops, then went to Kew Gardens. It was almost six when she finally made her way home, mingling with commuters as she used to do when she was working.

Karina caught her breath as the thought came to her.

She remembered the crowds, and she remembered hopping on and off buses. She concentrated hard as she tried to recall more, but nothing came. It was a start, though, another tiny fragment—like remembering the name Charles Forester and the fact that she disliked yellow roses. One day these pieces would become a whole. She would know exactly who she was and, more importantly, she would know whether Ford Fielding was telling the truth.

The phone was ringing as she got in and when she heard Ford's deep-timbred voice Karina felt a resurgence of the sensations following her dream. Her whole body sprang into tingling life. 'Ford.' She could not control a tremor in her voice.

'Are you all right, Karina?'

Heaven forbid that he knew what she was feeling. She swallowed hard and forced herself to become calm. 'Yes, of course, and thank you for the flowers. They were from you?'

'Who else do you know who would send you flowers?'

It was a light-hearted question but Karina gained the impression that he was holding his breath as he waited for her reply. She laughed. 'Oh, dozens of people. I get them all the time.'

He tried to match her laugh with one of his own, but he sounded oddly nervous. 'I was wondering, Karina, whether you would let me take you to the theatre tomorrow night?'

This was unlike Ford. Usually he would say, 'Come on, Karina, we're going out.' He would give her no choice, almost always making decisions for her.

'Well?' He sounded impatient for her answer.

'What to see?' Karina was afraid of sounding too enthusiastic. The truth was that she had missed him dreadfully, and hearing his voice on top of her dream made her doubly pleased that he had phoned.

'I thought *Buddy*. We never did get round to seeing it.'

'Yes,' she agreed. 'I think I'd like that.' There were several Buddy Holly CDs in the apartment which she sometimes listened to, and she knew from Ford that the singer had died tragically at the peak of his career in a plane crash. It would be an enjoyable evening—so long as Ford did not want more from her afterwards!

Despite her dream, despite her pleasure in hearing from him, she still only wanted friendship. It was too dangerous to commit herself deeply until her memory had fully returned.

'Good. I'll pick you up around seven. You're sure there's nothing wrong? You're coping on your own?'

'Perfectly,' she answered at once, adding with a laugh, 'I should have got rid of you months ago.'

'Karina!' He sounded dreadfully hurt. 'You don't mean that?'

'Idiot! I was joking. I couldn't have managed without you and you know it.'

'Till tomorrow, then?'

'Until tomorrow.'

Karina's legs were trembling when she replaced the receiver, and she wondered what was happening to her. All this because of a dream, and not even a dream about Ford. Some other man. Blond, Nordic-looking, with a good body and incredibly gentle hands.

Hands that could do anything, hands that could... Again she was twisting it around. Again it was Ford who was touching her. Was she going out of her mind? What was the matter with her?

For the rest of the day Karina was tormented by thoughts of two men, one black-haired, the other blond, both good-looking with fabulous bodies, and she was afraid to go to bed in case her dream recurred. In the end she had a dreamless night, and at seven the next evening she was ready and waiting when Ford came to pick her up.

For the first time since her accident he didn't let himself in. She waited a moment after he rang the bell, expecting to hear his key in the lock, but when it didn't happen she opened the door herself.

He was handsomer than ever. Most of the time he dressed in casual clothes, but this evening he wore a dark lounge suit and white silk shirt. They hid nothing of his powerful frame—rather they accentuated it. He took Karina's breath away, and it made her wonder why she'd never looked at him in this light before.

His eyes appraised—and sensitised—her, causing her breasts to harden beneath the oyster satin blouse, which she had teamed with a crystal pleated taupe skirt. Karina hid her feelings by turning to pick up her bag from the hall table next to the roses. 'I'm ready. Shall we go?'

Ford looked a little surprised that she hadn't asked him in but, nevertheless, he nodded. He had a taxi waiting outside, which took them to the theatre. They had a quick drink before the show and then were silent as they sat side by side, watching the performance.

Now and again he turned and smiled, as if assuring himself that she was all right, and in the interval they had another drink.

'Are you managing on your own, Karina?' he asked politely.

She nodded. 'Yes, thank you.'

'What have you been doing? Anything interesting?'

'Not really. Cleaning the apartment, going for walks, that sort of thing.'

'I see.'

'And I enquired about a graphic design course, but they don't start until September.'

His brows rose. 'You intend to go out to work again?'

'Of course.' She looked at him as though it had been a stupid question. 'I can't depend on you for ever.' As well as paying all the bills, Ford even gave her an allowance because she had no money. She had apparently withdrawn all but ten pounds from her account on the day of the accident. She had no idea why, and the police had drawn the conclusion that the youth responsible for snatching her bag—which had never been found—had watched her come out of the bank.

'Naturally,' he said quietly. 'And I'm sure it won't take you long to learn your job again.'

She had expected him to say that it wasn't necessary, that he would always look after her, and it seemed odd that he was agreeing with her.

It was as though he'd realised that he'd overstepped the mark before and was now on his best behaviour. But, in doing so, they had lost some of their easy familiarity which Karina felt was a shame.

Conversely, she was growing increasingly aware of him. Before her dream she had felt nothing. His kiss had started something, but it had been the dream which had wakened her emotions and had made her realise that she was capable of feeling far more for Ford Fielding than she had ever imagined possible.

Maybe things were stirring in her subconscious— maybe the love she had once felt for him was returning. It scared her a little, even though she knew she ought to be deliriously happy. She was the luckiest girl in the world to have someone like Stafford Fielding in love with her. Many girls would have scratched her eyes out to be her in her position.

Again they sat silent throughout the second half of the performance and, to her chagrin, Ford didn't even attempt to hold her hand. Not that she could blame him since she had set the rules. She ought to be pleased...

And yet she wasn't. She was inordinately hurt. She craved contact, needed it, yearned for it. And all because of her dream.

After the show Ford suggested they ate somewhere. 'We could go to my place,' he said, 'or wherever you prefer. We could even have a meal delivered to your apartment.'

Karina knew that if he took her home and continued to behave in this cool, polite manner, she would die of frustration, but neither did she want to go anywhere that was too intimate. 'We could go to McDonald's,' she said with forced cheerfulness. She missed the tightening of his lips, seeing only his shrug of acceptance.

'If that's what you really want. You never liked McDonald's before.'

'Didn't I?' She shrugged. 'I guess that's something else about me that's changed.'

Karina forced down her burger and chips because she knew that Ford would want to know what was wrong if she didn't, but all she could think about was Ford, making love to her.

The musky aftershave he wore was like an aphrodisiac. It enticed and provoked and she was consumed by spiralling emotions that seemed to drain the life-blood out of her body.

'You're very quiet tonight, Karina.'

'Am I? I was actually thinking the same thing about you.' It was another lie, but she could hardly say that she was busy fantasising about him making love to her.

'I thought there must be something wrong.'

'No, nothing.' She spoke sharply in an effort to combat the perverse need that was eating away at her. 'You're imagining things.'

'Am I?' he wanted to know. 'Then what's happened to our easy camaraderie?'

Karina's eyes flashed a vivid electric blue. 'I think you know the answer to that.'

His brows rose reprovingly. 'You're saying it's my

fault? That a couple of simple kisses has ruined our relationship for ever?' He sounded angry with her now.

'No, I'm not saying that,' she retorted. 'I *want* to be
friends with you. I want to get back on the same footing
as before.' She knew, however, that that was impossible.
Even if Ford made the effort she would never be able
to squash her own evolving sensuality. It would rise to
the surface every time they were together—and when
they weren't as well. Every time she thought about him,
in fact.

So why not let it? a tiny voice inside her asked. But
Karina knew that it didn't feel right. It had something
to do with her lost memory, something to do with their
argument when she had thrown her engagement ring
back at him. She'd thought a lot about him saying that
she'd had an affair, and was completely unable to come
to terms with it. Until she knew for sure what had happened she intended to keep her emotions well hidden.

'If you ask me, you're the one erecting barriers,' Ford
declared, his eyes cold, almost rejecting her.

Karina shivered. 'I beg your pardon?'

'All evening you've been shutting me out.'

'I don't think so.' She frowned, spoiling the arch of
her delicate brows. 'It's you who's been acting strangely.
I've never known you so remote before.'

'Only because I was picking up signals.'

'Then your antenna is wrongly wired,' she flashed
back.

'So what sort of signals should I have been receiv-
ing?'

Karina closed her eyes. Their sharp words were doing
nothing to stem her desire—quite the opposite. 'I think
I'd like to go home, Ford.'

'You'd rather not answer?'

'That's right,' she told him, and stood up.

Grim-mouthed, Ford followed suit, hailing one of the many black taxis cruising the streets. Neither spoke on the journey and Karina expected him to drop her off and then go home himself. Instead, he dismissed the cab and followed her inside.

The last time they'd been in this lift together, thought Karina, she had been in his arms, the beginning of the awakening of her senses. But tonight they stood in their separate corners like opponents in a boxing ring.

She stared straight ahead, and so did he, and the atmosphere was as thick as a pea-souper fog. When the doors opened she marched out first, then remembered that she hadn't brought her key and was compelled to stand back while Ford unlocked the door.

He led the way in and put on the lights, and as soon as she'd entered he closed the door behind her. It was their normal procedure yet tonight it all felt different, as though something major was about to happen.

She should, she knew, lead the way through and casually suggest coffee, as she always did, but for some reason she remained standing in the hall.

Ford faced her with his feet apart and his hands pushed into his trouser pockets, which should have made him look relaxed—but it didn't. His lips were pursed, his eyes narrowed and questioning. 'We seem to have a problem.'

Karina drew in a long unsteady breath. 'Yes.'

'But you don't want to tell me what it is.'

'No.'

'Are you calling an end to our relationship? You don't want me around any more? Is that it?'

'*No!*' It was an emphatic answer. Losing Ford was the last thing she wanted.

He frowned. 'Then what is it?'

'I want…' Her voice came out as a breathless whisper. 'I want us to remain friends.'

'I didn't realise that we'd fallen out.'

'I—I told you to go.'

'But I'm back again now—and you're the one erecting the barriers, not me. If you're suggesting that we get back on the same footing as before, I think that's impossible. You know it, and I know it.'

He looked at her long and hard and when she didn't speak he went on, 'I am, however, prepared to give you breathing space. I promised not to rush you. I think we need to begin all over again. It is why I sent the flowers, why I planned tonight most carefully. I—'

'That's part of the problem,' Karina cut in. 'You sent me roses, *yellow* roses, and you know I hate the sight of them because my mother…' Her voice trailed away.

'Your mother what?'

There was a long silence before Karina answered. 'I don't know. I don't know what I was going to say. I just know that I hate yellow roses—and that you, above all people, should have known that.' Tears were racing down her cheeks all of a sudden, and when Ford moved instinctively to take her into his arms she backed away.

In doing so she bumped into the table and the vase toppled and fell. Water and flowers spilled onto the polished wooden floor and glass shot in all directions.

In her anguish Karina snatched up most of the roses and threw them at him. 'Take these and go. I think you'll agree that they prove you and I have never had a serious relationship.'

CHAPTER THREE

THE best laid schemes of mice and men, thought Ford. Robert Burns had been right—they nearly always went astray. He had planned today so carefully, had been sure nothing could possibly go wrong. And now this.

The old Karina had most definitely loved yellow roses, but this new Karina was saying that she hated them. How had that happened? Did memory loss always cause such contradictory behaviour?

He knew now that his only chance was to reason with her. 'I'm not playing a game, Karina,' he said gently.

'Then what are you doing?' she demanded.

'I'm trying to win back the love of my fiancée.'

Karina held out her hand so that he could see her bare finger. 'I am not your fiancée.'

'What's in a ring?' Ford asked, his hands spread wide. 'You did agree to marry me. If we hadn't been so close how would I know so much about you?'

'I don't know,' she cried. 'I don't damn well know.' To his horror, tears filled her beautiful eyes. 'Everything I know is what you have told me. How do I know you haven't fed me a whole pack of lies?'

Ford shook his head. 'I've devoted the last twelve months of my life to you, Karina. Are those the actions of a man who's not in love? Who doesn't believe the girl he is helping is the woman he's going to marry?'

'I don't know. I don't know anything,' she insisted shakily.

'Come, Karina.' He held out his hands to her. 'Come

and sit down. Let me make you a cup of tea. And don't worry about this mess—I'll see to it.'

To his relief she allowed him to take her arm and lead her into the cheerful yellow sitting room. The old Karina had loved this room and had always laughed at the antics of the clowns which he had chosen so carefully, but the new Karina barely seemed to notice them, and they certainly never made her smile.

Once she was seated in a corner of one of the comfortable yellow and cream Regency stripe settees he put on the kettle and then began the task of sweeping up the remains of the crystal vase which he threw into the bin together with the flowers, all the time thinking what a disaster they had turned out to be. By the time he had finished the kettle had boiled.

Karina had watched him each time he walked through but she hadn't spoken or smiled. She seemed to be in a world of her own and he couldn't understand what was wrong with her. He wondered whether he ought to send for the doctor.

He poured the tea, handed her a cup, then sat back and waited silently. When she had finished and had put her cup on the table he spoke. 'Can't you tell me what is wrong, Karina?'

'There's nothing wrong,' she said quietly.

He shook his head. 'It's not what it looks like to me. First my kisses upset you, and now the flowers. Believe me, my darling, yellow roses *used* to be your favourites.'

Karina shook her head. 'I can't help that. All I know is that somewhere they hold bad memories.'

'You mentioned your mother. I thought she died when you were two?'

'I don't know why I mentioned her,' said Karina tetchily. 'Something made me do it but I don't know what. It's all such a muddle. If only I could remember.' She sank her head into her hands and willed herself to dig up memories.

'You know the doctor told you not to try and force anything,' Ford reminded her. 'It will happen in its own good time.'

'But it's been so long,' she insisted. 'OK, I know I've built a new life for myself, such as it is, but—'

'What do you mean, "such as it is"?' he enquired sharply. 'Aren't you happy? I've done my very best to—'

'Yes, I know,' she cut in tiredly, 'but I have no life beyond you. And that can't be right.'

Maybe he had been wrong, keeping her to himself. But she'd always seemed uncomfortable when he'd taken her out to meet other people so that in the end they had rarely visited and simply enjoyed each other's company.

He was sure she had enjoyed his. It was only in the last couple of days that there'd been a change in her. She was fine if he kept his distance, but the moment he tried to get any closer she backed off like a scared rabbit.

The contrast between this Karina and the pre-accident Karina was remarkable. Her sexual appetite then had been insatiable and she'd had a more vibrant personality too. He had loved her dearly—until he'd found out that she had been seeing someone else!

His lips firmed just thinking about it. He would never forget the day Geoffrey had told him that he'd seen Karina with another man.

'I'm telling you, Ford,' he'd said. 'They were all over each other like a rash. And this was in broad daylight. He dashed off in his Porsche afterwards and she stood and watched until he disappeared out of sight. She was well smitten, I can tell you. You'd be doing yourself a favour if you dropped her right now.'

'Are you sure it was Karina?' Ford had asked, finding it difficult to accept that she would have done something like that to him.

'As sure as I have a nose on my face. And it's not the first time I've seen them together either.'

Ford's face had darkened with anger. 'You never told me.'

'I was hoping I was wrong.'

'Dammit, man, you should have said something. She sure as hell is going to pay for this.'

Of course, when he'd confronted her she had denied it. She had accused him of not trusting her and had thrown her ring back at him.

And now she was letting him nowhere near her!

He should never have forgiven her. He should have washed his hands of her. He should never have gone to the hospital that night and should never have promised that he would look after her.

When she had walked out on him he had told himself that he didn't care, that he no longer loved her, that probably he never had, that their relationship had been based on a physical need and nothing else. He really had been prepared to dismiss her from his life.

It had only been his conscience that had made him go to the hospital, a feeling of guilt, of responsibility, a knowledge that it would never have happened if they hadn't fallen out.

But somehow the love that he felt for Karina now seemed different. Maybe it was the fact that he'd had to put his bodily needs and desires on hold that had made him see her in a new light. Or maybe she was different, too. She was gentler, often concerned about him and his feelings instead of always thinking about herself. She liked classical music instead of pop, quiet evenings at home instead of night clubs—that and a dozen other small things that he'd hardly noticed and yet which, when lumped altogether, made her an altogether nicer person.

As a consequence his love for this new Karina went very much deeper, and he knew that if she looked at him now and said, 'I love you, Ford, and want to marry you,' he would unequivocally forgive her affair with Charles Forester. He would make her his and they would spend the rest of their lives together.

Unfortunately, it was becoming increasingly clear that she would never do that, and it looked as though his plan to make her fall in love with him again was doomed before it started.

Never one to give up, though, Ford said quietly, 'It wasn't my intention to take over your life, Karina. I thought you needed me. Was I wrong?'

It was a long time before she answered, so long that he thought she wasn't going to answer at all. Then she said softly, huskily, 'No. I did need you.'

She'd used the past tense, he realised. 'But not any longer?'

'No—yes—oh, I don't know.'

Tears came again and this time he couldn't help himself. He gathered her to him and cradled her as if she were a child. He had to school himself hard not to give way to his rising desire. She needed comfort not kisses.

So it came as the devil's own shock when she said to him quietly, 'Kiss me, Ford.'

He looked down into the luminous blue of her eyes, saw the tremble of her lips, and the delicate flush on her cheeks. 'Are you sure?'

She gave a faint nod and his arms immediately tightened around her. She was so frail, so delicate, so lovely—so beautiful in every way.

With infinite slowness he lowered his head, and he could not control a groan of satisfaction as his lips met hers. But he was careful not to take more than she offered. He would let her set the pace—that way she could not accuse him of taking advantage.

Somehow, though, his good intentions fell by the wayside. The longer the kiss lasted the more rampant his male hormones became until it was impossible for him to master his desires.

His tongue took the place of his lips, tasting, stroking, creating powerful, electric emotions over which he was fast losing control. He felt her tremble, felt her sweetly scented body move against him, inducing a further urgency to his actions.

Heedless now of whether he was going too far, his hands brushed her breasts, breasts already hard and ripe for his touch, sensitised and throbbing, nipples thrusting against the shiny satin of her blouse.

He deftly undid buttons, pushed aside the lace of her bra and took her breast into his palm. He heard her gasp of pleasure, felt the arch of her body and every tremor that ran through her.

This was something he hadn't expected today, or for a long time, and all his pent-up emotions came clamouring to the surface in an explosion of feelings so intense he thought he was going to ignite.

He brushed the quivering tip of her breast with his thumb and felt fresh shivers of anticipation run through her. He heard her soft moans of delight, saw the way her head was flung back, her eyes closed, her whole body his for the taking.

He discarded her blouse completely, as well as her exquisite lace bra. He looked at her in aching wonder and touched both breasts at the same time, stroking, re-acquainting himself, marvelling at her beauty.

Then his head bowed and his tongue and teeth replaced his hands, and she cried out in fierce pleasure. She tasted beautiful, so erotically beautiful, better than he ever remembered. She was slightly smaller but that was understandable because she had lost weight after the accident, but she still had the power to twist every gut and sinew in his body. Oh, Lord, oh, Lord, oh, Lord. This was more than a man could stand.

He wanted more—he wanted to take her, make her his again. He wanted to eradicate the last twelve months and rediscover the mind-blowing pleasures they had once shared.

Karina knew that her battle was lost. She had fought to no avail and now the truth was staring her in the face.

She loved Ford Fielding.

It was a no-holds-barred love that didn't take into account that she didn't entirely trust him and wasn't altogether sure that she had ever been engaged to him. That was the disturbing factor. Up until then she'd never felt anything for him except gratitude and friendship. It would have made more sense had she immediately fallen in love with him again.

But the feel of his mouth on hers and the strong, exciting male taste of him drowned out these hesitant thoughts. She was aware only of pulses throbbing, of erotic sensations ripping through every vein and artery, of her heart trying to hammer its way through her breast-bone.

She couldn't contain the little sounds of pleasure from

deep in her throat, her own uninhibited response to his feverish kisses. She was in a world of sensation and uncontrollable urges.

She was aware of nothing except this moment in time, the feel of hot flesh against hot flesh, his arousal against hers, liquid fire shooting through her veins.

'Ford…' She gasped his name with no coherent thought to what she was saying. 'Oh, Ford.' His hand on her aching, swollen breast sent fresh agonising shudders through to the very heart of her, piercing her with pleasure.

'Karina, my very own precious Karina.' His voice was gruff and agonised, aching with intensity. 'It has been so long. I thought this day would never come.' His hand moved to her thigh, his gentle fingers inching their way upwards towards her moist, heated core.

Panic began to set in. This was more, much, much more than she'd anticipated when she'd asked Ford to kiss her. She wasn't even sure what had prompted her in the first place. Comfort maybe. She'd certainly not expected her own sizzling reaction—such an intensity of emotions, such deep, deep need, such fierce hunger. She wanted to open her body to him, to let him seek, take, satisfy.

But she had made a promise to herself that until her memory returned—until she was sure that Ford was who he said he was—she would not allow him to make love to her.

Even though you now love him? asked her inner voice.

Even though I love him, she answered sadly.

In desperation she jerked away, pushing herself up and moved on unsteady feet to the other side of the room to the window where she stared blindly into the inky jet of the night—anything but look into Ford's face.

He was hurt, she knew. She had glimpsed his astonishment and felt the way his body had stiffened, but she didn't realise how angry he was until he spoke. The roar of his voice made her jump.

'What the hell was that all about? You invite my kisses and then reject me. Is it a game? Or were you testing me? Checking to see whether my kisses are as good as your other lover's?'

The colour drained out of Karina's face. 'I don't know what you mean. There is no one else.'

'But there was.' His voice was bitingly cold and sharply condemning. 'Before your accident. And I suspect that you've now remembered it. So, tell me, how do I compare with Charles Forester?'

Charles Forester? Charles! A blond-haired, handsome face flashed before her mind's eye. Were they one and the same? Had she really and truly betrayed Ford's love?

An icy blast shivered across Karina's skin and she spun to look at him, her mouth and eyes wide. 'Is it true?' she whispered, her throat achingly tight, her whole body trembling.

'So you do remember,' he said scathingly. 'And, yes, it is true. I was prepared to forgive—until this little fiasco.' The fierce gitter in his eyes pierced her through and through until she winced with the pain of it.

Karina shook her head. 'You're wrong, Ford. My memory hasn't come back. And I'm quite sure that I would never be unfaithful. It's a gut feeling I have. I couldn't do that to you, not to anyone.'

'And I'm expected to believe that?' Contempt edged his voice. 'Tell me, Karina, why did you ask me to kiss you?'

She shook her head, her eyes hot with the effort of holding back tears. 'I don't know,' she whispered painfully.

'Don't know—or don't want to tell me?'

There was no letting up. His voice was still hard and accusing, his eyes condemning her, and Karina suddenly lost control. 'If this is how you see me then there's no point in us maintaining any sort of relationship. I feel as though you've stabbed me in the back. I never thought that possible of you. I looked up to you, I admired you, I was always grateful to you for your kindness. I—'

'But you never loved me.' Cynicism crept into his voice. 'You needed me because for some reason your lover never came to see you after the accident. What happened, I wonder? Had you fallen out with him as well?'

'Stop it! Stop it!' Karina clapped her hands over her ears, her cosy little world falling apart.

'Stop what? What am I doing?' he asked.

'You're threatening me,' she shot back. 'You're saying I've done things that I know nothing about. You're being viciously cruel. You're making me hate you.' She saw him flinch, saw a muscle jerk fiercely in his jaw, but she wasn't sorry—she was speaking the truth.

For over a year he had been the perfect gentleman and it was hard to believe that he was saying these harsh things to her now.

'Maybe I'm the one who should hate you, Karina.' His voice was silky smooth all of a sudden, his anger gone, something else she couldn't fathom taking its place.

'You're the one who ruined things between us,' he went on. 'Even if you can't remember—though I suspect that your loss of memory is very convenient at the moment—I can assure you that *I* do. And the pain when I discovered that you had been seeing someone else behind my back was something I never wish to experience again.'

Karina's tears finally overflowed, rolling hotly and slowly down her cheeks. She would never have done such a thing, she felt sure, and yet he was so convincing. 'If that is really what I did,' she said sadly, 'then I am sorry.'

'And that puts matters right, does it?' he asked with an odd flatness in his tone.

'Of course not,' she answered. If she had done what he was claiming then nothing could put it right. And it made his friendship and caring attitude since the accident all the harder to understand.

'Do you know something, Karina? There was a time when you would never have apologised to me. Argued, yes, denied, yes, but never apologised. If the accident has done nothing else it has changed you in that respect.'

Which one of me do you like best? she wanted to ask, but deemed it unwise. So much hung in the air between them, so much that was unpleasant. She would never forget this day as long as she lived, and the sooner she regained her memory and found out what had truly happened the happier she would be.

Whether she would like what she found was debatable. The thought that she had gone out with another man behind Ford's back sickened her. She simply couldn't imagine doing something like that. Yet there must be a grain of truth in it, otherwise why would she have dreamt about Charles Forester? Why would she have remembered his name?

And—more important—where did she and Ford go from here?

CHAPTER FOUR

KARINA writhed beneath Charles, fingers clawing naked skin, passion kindled to fever pitch, need overtaking discretion. When he finally entered her and when they reached their climax together wave after wave of the most achingly exquisite sensations shuddered through every inch of her.

It was not until he had made love to her for a second and then a third time, each with the same mind-blowing intensity, that Karina finally slept.

When she awoke, still with the aftermath of their love-making warming her, she discovered that it had been nothing more than another dream—a dream more intensely physical than her previous one, if that were possible. She could still feel Charles, touching her, inciting her to fever pitch, arousing her to unimaginable heights.

As before, with waking came the wish that it had been Ford who'd been making love to her, Ford who'd whispered those magical words of love, Ford's hands caressing, tormenting, inciting.

But she knew it could never be. By calling a halt to their love-making yesterday, she had effectively driven a wedge between them. Her alleged affair with Charles Forester had reared its ugly head again and Ford had walked out of her apartment, without making any plans to see her.

Her recurring dream disturbed her. Surely she wouldn't have dreamt so vividly about Charles if she hadn't known him, if they hadn't been lovers? Yet some-

thing deep in her subconscious still told her that this
could never be.

Confusion reigned in her mind once more, just as it
had in the days and weeks following her accident, and
she wished there was some way of accelerating her re-
covery. It was all very well for the doctors to tell her to
be patient, but for how long?

After a meagre breakfast of toast and tea she went out
to the shops to buy some bread, and as she waited to
cross the road she thought she saw Charles Forester on
the other side—or at least someone who looked very like
him, very like the man in her dream. It was a weird
feeling, recognising someone from her past, and she
couldn't be sure whether she was hallucinating or
whether it really was him.

Karina's heart pumped furiously and she called his
name but he didn't hear, and by the time she'd managed
to cross he had disappeared. She ran in the direction he
had taken but there was no sign of him and Karina grit-
ted her teeth in frustration. She wanted to shout out her
despair.

Charles could have filled in parts of her past that even
Ford could only have guessed at and it was infuriating
to have lost the opportunity. If it hadn't been for the
horrendous traffic she would have found out by now
whether she truly had had an affair with him or whether
Ford had been putting his own interpretation on things
that he didn't really know anything about.

She walked home slowly, her eyes searching all the
time in vain for the elusive Charles Forester. To have
missed him by only a few seconds was extremely an-
noying.

Not expecting to see Ford again—not for a while at
least—as he had left yesterday with his anger hidden

behind an icy front, it came as a profound shock when
he turned up an hour later.

As she looked at him and inhaled the musky male
smell which was his alone, scenes from her dream
flashed before her mind's eye—except that it was now
Ford who was making love to her, Ford who whispered
sweet nothings, Ford who aroused her to fever pitch. She
could actually feel herself sway towards him.

In her dream she had been lying on a sumptuous four-
poster bed in a high-ceilinged room, but now she had a
brief vision of the outside of the house—an impressive
porticoed mansion set in several hundred acres of park-
land.

Was it something else from her past? Charles
Forester's actual home? Had the dream, and seeing
Charles in the flesh this morning, unlocked another
memory? If it had, and if this was truly a place she knew,
then it looked as though Ford was right and that she had
been having an affair with him. The thought was deeply
disturbing.

'You look as though you've seen a ghost, Karina. Do
I upset you that much?' Ford spoke tersely, the scowl
on his face evidence that he was still very angry.

Her vision faded abruptly and she smiled. 'No, of
course not. I was thinking of something else.'

'Or perhaps *someone* else,' he said darkly. 'Perhaps it
was this someone you were expecting and not me.'

'I was expecting no one, and you know it,' she retorted, her blue eyes flashing defensively. She had been
going to tell him about seeing Charles but his harsh
words made her change her mind. 'I have some coffee
on—would you like a cup?'

'No, thanks,' he said, dropping into his favourite armchair and stretching out his long legs.

Karina sat as well, perching on the edge of one of the settees with her ankles neatly crossed. 'I really didn't expect to see you so soon. You were pretty mad with me yesterday.'

Ford's brows rose. 'What did you expect when you led me on then sent me crashing? You were always a tease, but you never cut me off in full flow before.'

A tease! Heaven forbid that she was that kind of girl. 'I hadn't intended to let things go that far,' she said quietly, her hands clasped in her lap, giving every outward appearance of being cool and calm while inside, with memories of the dream still vivid, her heart thudded painfully against her ribs.

This was the man Karina loved and who'd said that he loved her, and yet they were sitting here like strangers, stiff and remote, talking and yet revealing none of their real emotions—both acting a part. Why couldn't he understand that she needed to find her memory before she gave her body to him and admitted her love? Didn't he realise how important it was to her?

'Then you should never have invited me to kiss you.' He stared at her mouth as he spoke, as though wondering whether he dared kiss her again.

Karina's bones felt as if they were beginning to melt and she jumped to her feet. 'I'm going to have a coffee. Are you sure you don't want one?'

'Perfectly sure,' he said. 'Sit down, Karina. I came to apologise for throwing Charles Forrester at you. It was wrong of me. I know you can't remember him and I ought not to keep on…'

Now was the time to tell Ford that she'd seen Charles, but she didn't. She said instead, 'Do you know where he lives?' Immediately after the words were out Karina knew it had been the wrong thing to say. She could see the disbelief and anger rising up in Ford like a flash flood.

'It's not because I want to go and see him,' she added quickly, even though it was exactly what she wanted. Talking to Charles would surely settle the matter once and for all. 'A few minutes ago I had this picture in my mind's eye of a beautiful mansion, and I wondered if it was his, that's all.'

'And why would you think it belonged to Charles? Why would he be the first person who sprang to mind?' An icy stillness had come over him, his voice as sharp as the cutting edge of a sword, his face turned to granite.

He was condemning her before she could explain. Karina felt a surge of bitter resentment, and she certainly wasn't going to tell him about seeing Charles now.

'You can forgive but not forget, you told me, but it would appear that you're nowhere near to forgiving. *If* I had an affair with Charles Forester then at least the aftermath has taught me a thing or two about you. You can't resist turning the knife, can you? Every opportunity you get you ram Charles down my throat.' She shook her head angrily. 'I'm glad I fell out of love with you.'

Her barb hit home but the pain in his eyes was quickly masked. 'I still want to know why you thought the house might belong to Charles.' There was a cold flatness to his tone, worse than his anger, and it sent a shiver down Karina's spine.

'Because he's the only person I've remembered so far. And it was a big mansion. I assumed...'

'Couldn't it have been some stately home you once visited?' he asked shortly.

'I—suppose so,' she agreed.

'But you'd rather think it belongs to the man you left me for?' he added scathingly, eyes hard and blazing. He sprang up from his chair and faced her, like an enraged lion about to make its kill.

Karina rose also then stepped back a couple of paces, her chin high, her blue eyes fixed on his. She should have felt intimidated by him, and yet all she could think about was the feel of his mouth on hers, the gentle touch of his exploring hands, the liquid fire that ran through her veins. 'I can't imagine why you're so upset,' Karina said, looking straight into the cold hardness of his eyes. 'I thought you'd be pleased that I'd remembered something else.'

'Dammit, I am pleased.' Ford shook his head as if to clear it of all harsh thoughts. On a quieter note he added, 'I am, Karina. It's excellent news.'

But she knew that he was asking himself why she was remembering things to do with Charles and nothing to do with him.

Ford had the best intentions in the world when he'd come to the apartment. He'd spent a sleepless night, thinking about Karina and Charles, and knew that he shouldn't have brought the other man into the conversation. He'd been fully prepared to apologise this morning—until she'd asked him if he knew where Charles lived.

He'd seen red then. She couldn't have made her preferences any clearer. All the months he'd spent with her since the accident meant nothing. Not a thing. His patience had been rewarded with *this*.

Yesterday, when she'd begged him to kiss her, he'd thought that all his worries were over and had allowed his feelings to run free. He'd been totally unprepared, frozen into disbelief, when she'd called an abrupt halt.

The question now was did he give up? Did he fade

quietly into the background and let Karina pursue
Charles Forester? Or did he pull out all the stops and
persuade her to accept that she was still in love with
him?

It was not a hard decision. He loved her so much that
he knew he could never let her go. The subtle changes
in her since the accident—her gentler moods, the way
she reacted to certain situations, her tolerance and patience—both enchanted and delighted him. And he
would like to think that her affair with Charles had been
simply that—an affair.

If it had been physical feelings which had driven
her—although he could not imagine why when their own
love life had been so fantastic—he could only hope and
pray that they had burnt themselves out. Only time
would tell—except that his patience was in danger of
expiring. He had never expected that it would take her
this long to recover her memory.

Maybe he ought to give it a helping hand. Maybe the
doctors were wrong and he ought to encourage her to
remember. One or two things had started to come back
so why not more—with a little persuasion?

With a tremendous effort Ford pushed all thoughts of
Charles Forester from his mind. He took a deep breath
and he smiled. 'I think we should forget this whole thing.
I think I should take you out on another driving lesson.'

Karina looked at him warily but to his relief she
slowly nodded. 'I think I'd like that. I'm looking forward
to the day when I can drive on my own.'

So that she'd no longer be reliant on him? It was a
painful thought, but he continued to smile. 'We'll take
a picnic and make a day of it.'

'What a wonderful idea,' she said, smiling now as
though the suggestion really did appeal to her. 'Although

I don't think,' she added doubtfully, 'that I have very much in the fridge.'

'That's all right. We'll stop and buy whatever we need. Grab your bag and let's go.' He wanted to get out of the flat before she changed her mind. He had the whole day to put things right, to encourage a few more memories, but more than that—more than anything—he wanted her to fall in love with him again.

She'd said she was glad she'd fallen out of love with him and her words had cut deep. He had to prove to her that she was wrong—that she had never stopped loving him, that the Charles affair had been a temporary aberration—and that he understood and forgave her, even though she didn't seem to think he had.

They stopped to buy a whole cooked chicken, slices of ham off the bone, tomatoes and French bread, fruit, cheese and wine—simple food, but tasting like a feast if eaten with the right person in the right place. And he knew exactly where that place was.

Karina's driving was good. She had learned easily and was careful and considerate to other road users. She showed none of the impatience that she had exhibited in the past when she used to sound her horn unnecessarily when stuck in traffic or when someone did something stupid.

'You're doing really well,' he told her. 'I'm very proud of you. Turn left at the next junction.'

He saw Karina's happy smile and the way she seemed to sit that little bit straighter when he praised her. He enjoyed sitting and looking at her with her elegant, long-fingered hands on the wheel, hands which had touched him in so many different ways—excited him, aroused him, given him endless pleasure.

'Straight on at the lights.' He must remember to keep

his eyes on the road. Even the smell of her tormented him, a light floral fragrance that was different to anything she had worn before.

Her skirt had ridden up and as she pulled away from the traffic lights his eyes were drawn to the few inches of lightly tanned thigh. He wanted to touch her—push her skirt even higher. Oh, Lord, stop, he told himself sharply. This was no way to carry on when he was supposed to be giving her a driving lesson.

'Slow down,' he said. 'You're going too fast.'

'No, I'm not,' she told him in surprise. 'I'm doing just under thirty, and that's the limit. I've been watching the signs carefully.'

'Maybe it just seems fast,' he agreed. It was his own emotions which were running away with him, not the car. He kept his eyes on the road for the next few miles, issuing occasional instructions, but it wasn't long before his attention wandered again—to her mouth this time, her infinitely kissable, infinitely erotic mouth.

She was concentrating intently on her driving, unaware that her lips were parted and that occasionally the tip of her tongue ran across the edge of her teeth. Ford felt a wicked surge of his hormones and dragged his eyes away yet again.

They had been travelling for over half an hour when he directed her down a narrow country lane.

For the first time she showed curiosity. 'Where are we going?'

He smiled mysteriously. 'I know the perfect spot. Go carefully here—the road's very narrow.' They drove for another three miles along the narrow twisting lane, meeting no other traffic, until finally he told her to stop.

With Ford carrying the food and blanket, they climbed over a five-barred gate, walked through a wooded glade and trudged almost another mile until they reached the banks of a sparkling river with a tiny sandy shore and giant boulders that formed stepping stones to the other side. In the distance gently undulating hills were dotted with sheep and above them the sky was an incredible blue.

'Ford, it's beautiful.' Karina stood and looked around her, and he watched her changing expressions—pleasure, enchantment, sheer delight—but there was nothing to suggest that she remembered it.

His disappointment was so deep that he had to turn away and busy himself, spreading the blanket—anything but look at her and let her see the sheer torment in his eyes. He had been so sure that this was the one place that would trigger her memory.

'Have we been here before?'

Her tentative question had him whirling to face her, an expectant smile on his lips. 'You bet. It was one of our favourite places. Can you remember it?'

When she shook her head his heart sank like a lead weight in his chest. Although he tried to hide his disappointment, Karina saw it and said softly, 'Tell me about the times we've been here. Maybe I'll remember then.'

He drew her down onto the blanket and as they sat cross-legged, facing each other, her hands in his and his eyes intent on hers, he told her.

'The very first time I asked you out we came here. We went for a drive and a walk and came upon it quite unexpectedly, and after that it became our favourite get-away-from-it-all place. I guess we used to sit right about here.'

Karina looked down, as if trying to conjure up mem-

ories from this very spot, but when she looked at him
again her eyes were still blank.

'We caught a fish one day in the river—a tiny thing,
I admit—but we made a fire just over there and we
baked it in foil, and it was the best thing we'd ever
tasted.'

He waited for a flicker of awareness, but when there
was none he went on determinedly. 'And once, when we
were attempting to cross the river, you slipped off one
of the stones and fell into the water. When I gave you
my hand you pulled me in as well. You thought it a
huge joke.'

A smile tugged at Karina's lips. 'That was a bit
naughty of me. I hope it was a hot day.'

'It was,' he said. 'We stripped off our wet clothes and
hung them on the bushes to dry.'

'We sat around—naked?' she asked, sounding scan-
dalised.

Ford nodded. 'We didn't actually sit for very long.
We became rather amorous, as I remember, and ended
up making love—on this very blanket.' It had been one
of the most haunting experiences of his life. He could
remember every minute detail—the feel of her satin-
smooth skin as it dried quickly beneath the rays of the
sun, the fresh-air smell of her, the unforgettable taste of
her as his mouth and tongue explored.

As memories rose vividly, his mind overflowing with
them, Karina took her hands out of his. 'What if someone had come along and seen us?' she asked faintly,
making it sound as if it would have been the most dreadful thing in the world, although at the time she had
shown no such inhibitions.

'I knew they wouldn't. It's too far off the beaten
track.'

Without even seeming to realise what she was doing, Karina pulled her knees up her chin and wrapped her arms around them, as though even fully clothed she felt her nakedness, her vulnerability.

But Ford was still remembering that occasion because it had been the first time they'd made love. They had got near to it, yes, many times, but always he had held back. On this particular day, however, he had been unable to contain himself any longer.

A soft breeze had played on their skins, and the musical sound of the water and the singing of the birds had serenaded them. It had been perfect. She'd made no move to stop him when his exploring fingers had found her ready moistness, and when with a groan he'd raised his body over hers she'd flung her head back, wrapped her legs around him and arched herself in readiness.

He'd driven himself into her gently at first, but the sheer exquisite pleasure of her tightening around him had made his movements ever more urgent.

It had been over too quickly, her cries and his echoing in the hills surrounding them. Neither had wanted to move, each wanting to savour this closeness—this feeling of absolute rightness—in this joining of their bodies, this magical union.

He wanted to reach out for her now and recreate that wondrous occasion. He didn't like the way she had withdrawn from him, her body rejecting him. It was almost as though he had made matters worse by bringing her here and talking about making love.

'Karina.' He reached out and reluctantly she allowed him to take her hands again, trembling now as if she knew what a profound effect him making love to her had had on that particular day—but also as if she could not come to terms with it.

There was something else he had to tell her. 'It was also here, my sweetheart,' he said slowly and with a smile in his eyes, 'that you asked me to marry you.'

'*I* asked *you*?' Karina's eyes widened dramatically.

Ford nodded. 'You were a very liberated young woman, Karina. You didn't believe in beating about the bush. And I think that you'd got fed up, waiting for me to ask you.'

'So you said yes?' she asked huskily, looking positively shocked that she had done such a thing.

'Actually, I told you that I was a traditionalist at heart and that I should be the one doing the asking.'

'And did you?'

'Not exactly.' He remembered deciding that it didn't really matter, not when they were both so much in love.

'I'm sorry, Ford, I don't remember any of that.' Karina launched herself forward and buried her head in his chest, as though she found the ordeal of facing him too much to handle. 'I'm so sorry.'

Not as sorry as he was—or as disappointed. It pierced him with excruciating pain. He had been convinced that she would remember. How could she not? It had been such a momentous occasion. The two of them alone in the universe. Two insignificant people who had just made each other stupendously happy, who had promised themselves to each other, who were planning to spend the rest of their lives together.

How could she not remember?

He suddenly realised that tears were trickling down Karina's cheeks. 'Hey, baby, don't cry. It's all right.'

'No, it's not all right,' she whispered. 'It's not fair on you.'

'Don't think about me,' he said. 'You're the one who's being ravaged by all of this. I shouldn't have tried to force you into remembering. I should have been patient.' But, hell, how much longer did he have to wait? Could his body stand it? To hold her in his arms, without kissing her, without touching her or tasting the sweetness of her, was driving him insane.

From somewhere he found an inner strength. He pulled out a clean linen handkerchief and gently mopped her face. When it was dry he said, 'I think maybe we ought to get on with our picnic.' Although, if he was honest, he didn't feel in the least like eating. And he was quite sure that Karina didn't either.

Somehow both of them managed to eat some food and they drank all the wine, and afterwards he suggested they went for a walk.

They used the stepping stones to cross the river. Ford wanted to point out where she had fallen but thought it wiser not to in the wake of her withdrawal, but he showed her a cave where they had once sheltered during a storm. 'You lost an earring here,' he told her, 'and we came looking for it months later and it was still where it had fallen.'

'Incredible,' she murmured, but she seemed a million miles away from him and he wondered what she was thinking.

Eventually, in silence, they made their way back to the car, and when he asked Karina if she wanted to drive she shook her head.

'I'm sorry if the day hasn't been a success,' he said when they were seated. 'I thought it was a good idea. It would appear I was wrong.'

'It was a success,' she assured him. 'It's not your fault I can't remember things. It hurts me when I have to tell you I can't. I want it more than you do. It's so fiercely frustrating. There are times when I could sit in a corner and scream.'

Ford winced and, half turning in his seat, he placed his hand over hers. 'You make me feel very humble. I have no right to ever be angry with you. None at all. You must be living in hell. All I hope is that I've made the last twelve months in some small way bearable for you.'

Her eyes misted. 'In more than a small way, Ford. You've been my entire life. I could never have coped alone.'

'And can I go on, being your entire life?' He held his breath as he posed the question. He knew he was treading on dangerous ground. What he would do if her answer was no he had no idea. Perhaps he shouldn't have asked.

Her incredible blue eyes were sad as she looked at him. 'If I lost you, Ford, I would have no reason to go on living. There might be times when I tell you to get out of my life—that I want some space, that I want to be alone, that I want independence—but it's not really true.'

It made his heart sing to hear her say that. 'You really mean it?'

'From the bottom of my heart. You've been a very dear friend to me and I want it to continue that way.'

Some of his joy faded. He wanted to be more than a friend. He wanted to be her lover and, more important, her husband.

Was that never to be his role in life now? Had he lost her for ever? The more time went by the more Ford began to think that there was a distinct possibility she would never regain her memory. With Karina saying that she couldn't get on with her life until she did, what sort of a penance was she forging for herself? And for him, too? It did not bear thinking about.

He drove home deep in thought, unconsciously heading to his own Hampstead house instead of Karina's apartment. It was not until he pulled up outside that he realised what he had done.

Why had Karina said nothing, he wondered, until he glanced across and saw that she was asleep. Or at least her eyes were closed. She opened them when he cut the engine and she looked about her with a frown. 'What are we doing here?'

He had to be honest. 'I don't know. I came home on automatic pilot. But the least we can do is have a cup of tea now we're here, don't you think?'

Karina nodded, though she didn't look very happy about it.

He'd brought her here only once since her accident and she'd stood in awe as she'd gazed at the immense rooms with their high, gilded ceilings, the beautiful pieces of furniture, glowing with the patina of age, the crystal chandeliers and the priceless paintings. 'You live *here*?' she'd asked in a hushed voice.

He'd smiled proudly. 'Indeed I do. What do you think of it?'

'I think,' she said slowly and honestly, 'that it's overpowering. I could never live somewhere like this. I feel much safer in my apartment.'

When he'd asked her to define the word 'safer' she'd said, 'It's cosier, it's warmer, it's home.'

He'd been tremendously disappointed but at the same time he'd understood her feelings. The flat was the only home she knew, her bolthole from the unknown, terrifying outside world. It afforded her the same sort of security she had once felt in her mother's womb. There had been so much for her to learn in those first few months, so much to understand, to question, to accept. And his grand Georgian home had intimidated her.

Ironically, before she'd lost her memory Karina had thought it a wonderful place. She'd said she would be proud to live here and show it off to all her friends. He'd had a moment's doubt when she'd said that, and had wondered whether it was the trappings of wealth that had attracted her rather than himself. He'd dismissed the thought instantly and had begun to imagine her in an elegant evening gown, descending the wide staircase and dazzling him—as well as all his guests—with her beauty.

So it was with some hesitation that he led Karina in now.

CHAPTER FIVE

KARINA wished Ford hadn't brought her here to this mansion that, in her opinion, was an ostentatious show of wealth. It was sinful for one man to live alone in such a huge place.

He hadn't told her how he had acquired it—whether it had been in the family for generations or whether he had bought it in recent years with profits from his business—and she hadn't asked because she didn't like the place. It was far too grand.

She knew he was an only child, and that both his parents had died in a tragic boating accident when he was fourteen. He had been looked after by his paternal grandfather until he was eighteen—the only one of his grandparents still alive—and then Grandpa Fielding had died and Ford had been left on his own.

He'd left school straight away, instead of going on to university as he had originally planned, and got a job in the computer industry. A few years later he'd decided he'd had enough of working for someone else and had set himself up in business, selling software—a lot of which he wrote himself. His business had flourished and he'd expanded into hardware and peripherals and now had at least forty people working for him.

Karina accompanied Ford through the oval hall with its Doric columns and its plasterwork frieze and its Greek statues set in niches. It was like a museum, she thought, and extremely chilly despite the warmth of the day. They went down endless corridors until they reached the kitchen, which to her relief was flooded with late afternoon sunlight.

Ford filled the kettle and she asked where his house-keeper was.

'Molly's on her annual holiday,' he explained, 'one I always have to force her to take. She thinks I can't look after myself.'

Karina knew that he also had an army of people who cleaned and cooked and gardened and generally kept the place in good order. Today, though, all was still and silent and she wished that she'd insisted on him taking her home.

They talked desultorily while he made the tea and then he took it outside into a tiny sheltered courtyard with a fountain in the centre and a curtain of roses covering the walls. They sat on a padded bench in a niche in the wall, the tray on a stone table in front of them.

She helped herself to a slice of home-made ginger cake, which was sweet and sticky and entirely delicious, but it wasn't until she licked her fingers afterwards that she saw Ford watching her. The desire in his eyes sent a flood of warmth rushing across her skin.

'I'm sorry,' he said. 'I should have provided you with a napkin, although I have to confess that seeing you lick your fingers is infinitely more—interesting. Actually, I could have done it for you.'

And turned the whole thing into an erotic game, thought Karina unhappily. Was he never going to give up? Couldn't he accept that she still needed time, before letting their relationship develop into something deeper?

Even as these thoughts ran through her mind her whole body was a mass of sensation. It responded so completely to him these days that it was becoming harder and harder to pretend indifference. While her

head saw the sensible side of things her heart knew that
she found Ford Fielding wildly attractive.

She picked up her cup and tried to hide behind it—
without any success. Ford was still watching her, still
had a hungry look in his eyes. The instant she had drunk
her tea and put her cup down he reached across and
touched the curve of her cheek.

'What are you looking so worried about, sweetheart?'

'I'm not worried,' she announced, shocked to hear the
huskiness in her voice. She could feel every part of her
respond to his touch, melting under an impossible heat.

'I think you are.' Ford's eyes moved to the frenzied
pulse at the base of her throat. 'Was it me telling you
that we'd made love in the open air.'

'I can't imagine I would ever do something like that,'
she told him quietly—determinedly prim.

'With the right man, in the right mood, I think you
would.' His voice had lowered to a growl, his eyes dark
and hooded so that she could no longer see the desire
lurking there. But she knew it hadn't gone away, and
the longer he continued to look at her, stroking, tormenting, the more agitated she became.

'Ford, please, don't touch me like that.'

'Like what? What am I doing?'

But she knew that he knew, and his fingers moved
slowly along the curve of her throat, finding the tell-tale
pulse. All the time his eyes were on hers, judging her
response—knowing her better than she knew herself.

He shifted closer and gently held her against him—
against the hardness of a body that was as overheated as
her own. He slid one arm around her shoulders and his
other hand lifted her chin, compelling her to look at him.
'Can't you feel the electric current that runs between
us?' he asked fiercely. 'The heat that melts our bodies

and binds us inexorably? We belong together, my own sweet darling—we always have done, we always will.'

Such confidence shook her. 'Things have changed,' she cried out desperately. 'It might have been true once, but—'

His possessive mouth cut off her words as he claimed her lips with a groan of satisfaction. When she put a hand to his chest to push him away she felt the urgent thud of his heart, and knew that if she didn't call a halt immediately things would very easily get out of control.

Her own tortured body would let her down. It would respond with throbbing intensity to his demands—take what was offered and give equally in return. It would betray her innermost secret.

'You can't stop the inevitable,' he muttered, his voice thick with emotion.

Somehow Karina managed to pull herself out of his embrace and stand up, but he was on his feet at once. He caught her shoulders and propelled her back a step until she was against the wall, held captive by his body.

She took a deep, unsteady breath and closed her eyes, her limbs rigid and her hands clenched into fists at her sides.

'Sweetheart, don't fight me.'

She heard his throaty voice closing in on her, felt his breath against her cheek and then his mouth took hers in an urgent, demanding kiss. There was nowhere to run, nowhere to hide. He had made her his prisoner, his hard body against hers, his hands moving from her shoulders to her hips to mould her body to his and make her feel how great was his arousal.

'I can't get you out of my mind,' he murmured hoarsely. 'I can't let you go, not ever.'

Their hearts pounded in unison and Karina knew it

was going to be extremely hard, if not impossible, to remain indifferent. Had he been gently persuasive she might have done so, but this fierce hunger, this desperate need—this yearning of body and soul—that was overtaking him was too much to deny.

It was sweeping her along on a tide of emotion. Sensations hurtled through every inch of her body at breakneck speed, consuming her, sensitising her, spinning her out of this world and into another where only feelings mattered.

Because she was afraid of what was happening to her, she said the only thing that she knew would stop him. 'In spite of Charles?'

She felt the stillness that came over him and heard his swift intake of breath, but he didn't withdraw or abuse her with angry words. Instead, he said in a voice filled with raw emotion, 'In spite of Charles. I can forgive you anything, my sweetheart. I *have* forgiven you. I've spent long, empty, sleepless nights, thinking of nothing but you and what you mean to me. You are a part of me, Karina. I hope you can accept that. All I want is for us to be together for all time.'

When his lips closed on hers yet again Karina bowed both to his will and to the dictates of her own heart, returning his kisses with a sudden passion that left Ford in little doubt as to her feelings.

With a groan his arms tightened about her. His kisses became more desperate, his mouth devouring hers, his fierce need spiralling her into further pinnacles of sensation.

There was no turning back now. She had given him hope, a sign that maybe, after all, her love for him could be revived. His body swayed against hers and Karina unconsciously urged herself rhythmically against him.

Only a short time ago she had prudishly declared that she would never make love on a blanket under the skies, and yet she knew now that if she were feeling like this at the time then she might have different ideas. Her stomach was a churning mass of sensation which soon spread to every corner of her body. And the heart of her, the woman's heart of her, was on fire with need.

She had never felt like this before, at least not since her accident, and it was a new and wondrous experience. It was not until Ford took her hand, with the intention of leading her back inside the house—and very probably up to his bedroom—that she shook her head and came one step back down towards earth. 'Please, Ford, let's take things slowly. I need time to get used to the idea that—'

'That you love me,' he finished for her. 'There was never a doubt in my mind—and I'm sure not in yours either if you're honest with yourself.' He looked at her speculatively. 'But I will bow to your wishes as long as I know that there is now light at the end of the tunnel.'

'I know what you do to me,' she whispered achingly. 'I'm not sure whether it is love.'

Ford smiled knowledgeably. 'Believe me, my sweet, it *is* love. You've proved to me that it has to be all or nothing.' He paused and looked thoughtful for a brief moment. 'That again is part of the new you. Your very reluctance to enter into any sort of relationship until you are sure of your feelings does you much credit.'

'You mean I wasn't like that before?'

'I'm afraid not, Karina. You were a very highly sexed individual who—'

'I don't think I want to hear any more,' she cut in quickly. 'I don't think I like the person I was.' She found the whole situation distressing. Could a knock on the head really change a person's personality? Had she really been something of a sex fiend? The very thought flushed her skin with embarrassing heat.

'Karina, sweetheart, please don't think like that. There was nothing wrong with you. You were a—'

'I think I'd like to go home,' she said abruptly.

'As you wish.' Ford looked desperately disappointed and she wanted nothing more than for him to hold her and console her, but she knew where it would lead. After what he'd told her she knew it would be a long time before she let him kiss her again.

It was totally shameful that she had once thrown herself at him and that sex had been one of her highest priorities. There was a whole world of difference between making love and having sex, and if that was the sort of person she was then she hated herself.

Ford picked up the tray and took it into the kitchen. Karina followed him miserably. 'You really ought not to think harshly of yourself,' he told her, as he began to load their cups and plates into the dishwasher. 'There's nothing wrong in being highly sexed as long as it forms part of a loving relationship.'

'And that's what we had?'

'Most definitely. You loved me and I was crazily in love with you.'

'And now?' she asked quietly, wondering how he could love the sort of person she had become if she was so different from before.

'I love you more than ever. Actually, it's like loving a different woman, and you are wonderful.' He held out his hands and reluctantly she took them. 'You are my sunshine, my moon, my stars, all rolled into one. You are my entire world, Karina. You are my universe. You must never doubt that or forget it.'

'But if I'm so different I don't see how...' Words failed her. What could she say, how could she explain her humiliation?

'The change in you is for the best, my sweet darling. I love you more now than I ever did. Does that answer your question?'

Karina closed her eyes as a tremor ran through her and she felt herself being pulled insistently against him to feel once again the heat of him, the masculine hardness, the desire which he had kept under control for so very, very long. The heady, musky smell of him, which was so essentially Ford, drugged her senses to such an extent that when he lowered his head to seek her mouth cautiously she could deny him nothing.

There was no hunger in his kiss this time. There was love and reassurance and patience, and understanding of this new set of emotions that had taken her by surprise.

He cupped her face with both hands and she was driven to look into the velvet darkness of his eyes. She saw pain there, but hope too, and she leaned her head against his chest and let him hold her.

Her eyes felt moist and her heart had begun a new race against itself. Whatever she had been like before—whatever she was now—she knew that she loved this man with every fibre of her being, and that it would be only fair to tell him so.

The clamour of a bell rang loudly above the kitchen door. There was a whole row of bells, each a different colour and connected to different rooms in the house, left over from a previous era but still in working order. This was the main door, however, and Ford frowned harshly at this rude interruption at such a private moment.

'I'll be as quick as I can,' he announced gruffly, his own emotion still very much to the fore.

'You could ignore it,' she whispered, her hands on his arms, checking him. 'No one knows we're here.' If he disappeared, if only for a few seconds, she knew that this rare mood when she truly wanted to bare her soul would be gone for ever.

'Is that what you want?' He looked at her questioningly, wonderingly.

Karina inclined her head, and whispered one word. 'Yes.'

So he stayed where he was. The bell rang one more time and then was silent. Karina lifted her chin to look at him and his mouth claimed hers.

Again there was no sense of urgency, no sign of the deep hunger that she knew he felt. He was aware of a need to pace himself carefully if he didn't want to scare her away.

Instead, it was Karina who took the initiative, running the tip of her tongue over his lips and invading the mysteries of his mouth. Karina who moved her hips with unconscious eroticism against him. Karina who unbuttoned his shirt and slid her fingers over the hair-roughed skin of his muscular chest. Karina who took his nipples between thumb and forefinger and felt the shudders of pleasure ripple through him.

She had been scarcely conscious of his quiet moans, aware only of the pleasure that she herself was deriving from her completely alien actions. Finally he could control himself no longer and uttered out loud, 'Oh, Karina, in heaven's name, what are you doing to me?'

His voice, reaching somewhere into her subconscious, snapped Karina out of her self-induced trance. 'I—I'm sorry,' she began.

'Lord, don't be sorry. This is wonderful, this is what I've been waiting for. This is more like—'

Karina pulled back, her face flaming. 'More like how I used to be?' Instead of accepting that this was how people reacted to love—that it was a perfectly natural way to behave—she felt nothing but revulsion.

She swung away from him, trying to keep her head high and the pain out of her voice. 'This is what you like, is it—girls who fling themselves at you? Girls who—?'

'Good Lord, no, Karina. You're mistaken.'

He touched her shoulders and tried to turn her to face him but she pulled away angrily, though she had to concede that she was more angry with herself than with Ford. Had she told him that she loved him before it had happened it would have been different, but to behave so wantonly without those magic words having been spoken was madness in itself.

'I want to go home, Ford.'

He gave a faint nod, knowing that this time she really meant it and that nothing he could say would make her change her mind.

Ford lay and stared at the ceiling, wide awake even though he had been in bed for several hours. What a disastrous day, and what a fool he had been. He knew only too well that Karina needed to be persuaded and coaxed, not forced into a relationship she wasn't ready for.

Why had he been so persistent? What had happened to the patience that had stood him in good stead for so long? The answer was simple. He had come to the end of his tolerance. He had reached his breaking point. No longer could he sit back and wait for things to happen. He needed to *make* them happen.

Karina hadn't even asked him in when he'd taken her back to her apartment. She'd coolly said goodnight and he had no idea when he would see her again. It would be up to him, he knew that, but how many times could he try? How many times could he stand up only to be knocked down again?

It was so maddeningly frustrating. Even thinking about Karina sent rampant hormones chasing around his body. She was so beautiful, so perfect. He could almost feel the silkiness of her long black hair and the velvet softness of her skin. He even imagined that he could smell the fragrance of her body and feel her unconscious sensuality.

His heart pounded, his hands reached out and touched—nothing. He swore and bounced out of bed. This was madness. This was sheer insanity. He could wait for ever at the rate he was going and his body just couldn't stand it any more.

He'd had enough. Karina had made it clear that there was never going to be anything more than friendship between them—and he couldn't handle it any longer. He wanted all or nothing. If it was nothing then he should forget her and start a new life for himself, dating other women. He'd done his duty, more than could be expected of him. The time had come to close these chapters in his life. It was an unhappy ending to the story—but he had no other choice.

His mind made up, Ford expected to feel better, but he didn't. He felt ten times worse. He loved Karina desperately, far more than he had in the past, and giving her up was going to be well nigh impossible. He intended to attempt it, however, no matter how hard it was.

After taking his second shower of the evening, he got back into bed and once more tried to sleep.

He had just dozed off when the sound of the telephone woke him. Cursing furiously, he picked up the receiver from the side of the bed and snapped, 'Yes?' The glowing red numbers on his clock told him that it was a little after two.

'Ford, it's me.'

Karina's scared little voice made him sit bolt upright, and he clicked on the bedside lamp as he spoke. 'What's the matter?' All sorts of alarming thoughts ran through his mind. 'Karina? Tell me.' Not a burglary, not an assault, not something physical please, God.

'I couldn't sleep and I went to get a drink and I fell down the step into the kitchen. I think I've sprained my ankle.'

He wanted to laugh with pure relief because if anyone had laid a hand on her...

'I can hardly walk. I didn't want to bother you but it hurts like hell and—I didn't know who else to ring.'

She sounded penitent as though she ought not to have got him out of bed, but, Lord, he was glad that she had. If she'd rung the doctor or the hospital and sorted it out herself he would have been as mad as hell. 'Karina, I'll be there as soon as I can.'

He threw on his shirt and trousers, socks and shoes, and in less than a minute was unlocking his car, glad that for once he'd left it out, instead of garaging it.

He completed the journey in record time and found Karina lying on the settee with her feet up, her face devoid of all colour.

'You poor darling,' he said.' I think I should take you to the hospital and let them X-ray it just in case you've broken anything.'

Without waiting for any objections, he lifted her in his arms, still in her nightdress and dressing-gown, and sent up a silent prayer of gratitude that he was being given the opportunity to play nursemaid again. Maybe this time, with a stroke of luck, he would manage to persuade her that she did, indeed, love him.

The intoxicating scent of Karina as he held her close was enough to drive him crazy. To hell with the fact that it was a good Samaritan act—he wanted her. His groin ached with need and it was all he could do not to kiss her, not to hold her so tight that she would cry out with even more pain.

He looked down at her face but her eyes were closed and he guessed that she was thinking of nothing except her painful ankle.

The hospital confirmed that she had chipped a bone as well as having torn some ligaments, and her leg was put in plaster up to her knee, with only her toes peeping out. She was to return in six weeks to have it taken off.

They gave her a pair of crutches but Ford insisted on carrying her out to his car. He didn't like to think of Karina hurting herself, but inwardly he was delighted that he was being given another chance to spend time with her.

'I'm so sorry for being such a nuisance,' she said, as he lowered her gently into the passenger seat and then got in beside her.

'Sweetheart, don't ever think that.' He started the engine and slowly drew out of the almost deserted car park.

'But I got you out of bed in the middle of the night,' she protested, her blue eyes huge in her still pale face.

'And you think that I object? My darling, you should know that nothing is too much trouble where you are concerned. Compared to the trauma of your other accident, this is trivial.'

'But I seem to be making a habit of hurting myself,' she said wryly, 'and you're always the one left to pick up the pieces. I don't know how I'm ever going to repay your kindness.'

'There is a way,' he told her quietly, feeling the heavy beat of his heart as he waited for her response. He was going to take a gamble here—but if the answer was what he wanted it would be worth it.

'There is?' She looked at him expectantly, her blue eyes wide and innocent, unaware of the bombshell he was going to drop.

'Yes, my sweet. One eminently satisfactory conclusion.' His hands tightened on the steering-wheel. 'You could marry me.'

CHAPTER SIX

KARINA wished Ford hadn't said that. It wasn't the time, it wasn't the place. She hadn't told him yet that she loved him. It needed to be said before any proposal of marriage. Her foot throbbed and her head ached, and she didn't want to have to deal with this problem.

She was silent for so long that Ford spoke again. 'Not a good idea, eh?' She heard the disappointment in his voice.

A very bad idea, she wanted to answer, but didn't. She had spent hours thinking about the way her body ran amok when it was anywhere near him, the way her adrenalin surged and made it impossible to deny her depth of feelings—but she hated the idea that he thought her highly sexed.

She would never trade sex for love, not ever. If that was the type of person she had once been then she didn't think very much of herself—and would never go back to that way of life. If that was the type of person Ford preferred then he was asking her to marry him for all the wrong reasons—except that, maybe, just maybe, she was being paranoid.

'Am I not going to get a response at all?' Ford's quietly anxious voice penetrated her thoughts.

'You've taken me by surprise,' she said equally quietly, searching for the right thing to say which would not hurt him too much. It wasn't easy. Any response except an affirmative one would hurt.

There was no getting away from the fact that he was

a nice person and she was desperately in love with him, but she needed to tell him so in her own time when things were right for her. It had almost happened yesterday but it hadn't, and she might not now find the right moment until her memory returned. That would be the best time—when she knew herself again.

It was a crazy situation, and one she wouldn't wish on her worst enemy. No one knew the torment she suffered because her past life was an empty canvas. No matter what she was told about it nothing compensated for the fact that she *couldn't remember*.

Ford glanced at her and smiled wryly, trying his hardest not to look hurt or unduly anxious. 'A simple yes will suffice.'

Karina shook her head slowly and sadly. 'You know I can't do that, Ford. Not yet, anyway.'

'But there is hope?'

Not wanting to let him down any more, she whispered, 'Maybe.' She added, even more faintly, 'In the long term.'

She didn't look at him but was aware that his hands gripped the wheel a bit tighter. She guessed that his face was grim too. His jaw would be set and his eyes would be masked, revealing nothing of his torment.

She felt the need to say something more. 'Ford, you've always known that I want to get my memory back first.'

He didn't speak but he nodded, and she went on. 'It's very important to me.'

'And if you *never* get your memory back?'

Karina grimaced. 'I refuse to entertain that thought.' It was something that troubled her—something she dared not dwell on—but she wasn't going to admit it to Ford. The fact that she'd had a few flashes of memory led her to hope that before too long everything would fall into place.

She was clinging to that belief and if Ford was not prepared to wait then he knew what he could do—but she knew that he would be around for a while longer at least. He wouldn't leave her to fend for herself while her ankle was in plaster, even though it didn't really make her an invalid. Karina knew—and she felt sure that Ford knew also—that she could cope on her own if she had to.

He said no more and soon they reached her apartment. Once inside he fussed around her like a mother hen and ushered her back to bed and tucked her in, making sure there was nothing she wanted.

'I'll be in the other bedroom if you need me,' he told her gruffly.

'You don't have to stay, Ford.' Karina looked at him with worried blue eyes. The situation between her and this man seemed to get more complicated with each passing day. Here she was, desperately wanting his body and yet rigidly denying herself. He had no idea of the way her heart had thumped when he'd lifted her into bed—which he hadn't needed to do but he'd insisted—of the mountains of desire, creating chaos in the pit of her stomach, of her racing pulses at the thought of him sleeping in the next room.

Admittedly, he'd slept there for months after her accident, but she hadn't felt any love for him then—which made a big difference. He'd been a friend, a comforter, a nurse. Now he was a sexy male animal who had the power to disturb her, by merely looking at her.

As he was now. He was hovering at her bedside and those incredible dark eyes were raking her face, trying to read her thoughts—trying to probe the deepest recesses of her mind. 'You surely don't think that I would leave you to cope alone?'

'Of course not.' With great deliberation Karina pulled the sheets up around her chin and closed her eyes. 'I'm tired, Ford.'

The only warning she had that he was going to kiss her was when she felt the warmth of him close to her face. She braced herself for the onslaught, but was perversely disappointed when he did no more than briefly touch his lips to her forehead.

She wanted more—she clamoured for more—and it was all she could do not to pull her arms from beneath the bed cover and wrap them around his neck.

'Sweet dreams, little one.'

The huskiness of his voice gave him away, telling her that his need was as great as her own—that he was also having difficulty, keeping his hands off her.

She waited until the door closed, before opening her eyes. She'd never felt less like sleeping. It was almost as though fate was saying that they should not be apart. He had come running after her when she'd had her first accident, even though she had just broken their engagement, and now this further incident had brought him running again. It surely must tell her something.

Looking at the situation logically, it made no sense to keep him at bay. She loved him, he loved her, so why hold back?

You know why, a voice said inside her head.

Yes, but I feel as though I've been bulldozed into this relationship. It's not my own choice.

So whose choice is it?

Karina couldn't answer. She'd had every opportunity to tell Ford to go but she'd preferred to let things slide, to let things happen, until finally—this. Even though she

now knew for sure that she was in love with Ford she
still hung back, afraid to make a commitment in case it
was the wrong one.

But what could go wrong?

At worst her memory would return and she would find
that she had never loved Ford or that she had fallen out
of love with him because she'd loved Charles Forester
more. Either way, did it matter when she loved him
now? She was making the situation more difficult for
herself than it really was.

Sleep still eluded her and she lay there until the first
fingers of dawn began to streak the sky. She listened for
sounds of Ford but heard nothing. Obviously he had
dropped straight off to sleep and she felt irritated that he
was able to relax when she couldn't.

Her ankle wasn't hurting so much now and she swung
her legs out of bed. Scorning her crutches, she limped
to the window.

Almost as though he had been listening for her to
wake, Ford tapped on the door and entered. His smile
changed to a frown when he saw the crutches still at the
side of the bed where he'd left them for her convenience.

'Karina, what are you doing?' His tone was sharp.

'I can't sleep.'

'That's no excuse for not using your crutches.'

'They're too damned awkward,' she retorted crossly.

'You'll get used to them. You're not supposed to walk
on your foot yet.' On a softer, kinder note he asked,
'Shall I make you a cup of tea?'

She nodded, recalling the countless cups of tea he'd
made her when she'd first come home from hospital. It
was almost like a replay, except that there had been
nothing but kindness and patience and friendliness
then—none of this simmering sexuality.

By the time he returned Karina had composed herself. Even when he sat next to her she managed to maintain an outward appearance of being calm, despite the fact that all he wore was a pair of cotton trousers and his magnificently muscled chest with its thatch of dark hair tempted her to touch it.

'Does your foot hurt? Is that why you can't sleep? Can I get you a painkiller?'

He was being so attentive, so concerned, so polite, that she wanted to scream and say, no, just kiss me— that will make me better.

He would be perfectly willing to oblige, she knew, but it wouldn't be a solution to her problem—it would only add to it. Maybe she was doing the wrong thing, waiting for her memory to return before making a final commitment. Considering the depth of her feelings for him, what did it matter?

There was Charles Forester, of course. If she *had* left Ford for him, what would her feelings be towards Charles once her memory was restored? Would she again prefer this other man? It seemed impossible. How could she love anyone more than Ford? He was so wonderful in every respect. She couldn't imagine how she had fallen out of love with him in the first place.

Her confused thoughts must have reflected in her face because Ford said, 'You look deeply troubled, Karina. Is it the thought of having me around you again? If that's so then—'

'No!' She said the word instinctively. 'I don't mind you staying here—really.'

'Then what's troubling you?'

'It's nothing. I guess I'm annoyed with myself for being so clumsy. Just as I've become independent this has to happen.'

She could see that he didn't believe her, that her words hadn't matched her changing expressions, but he merely nodded as though he understood. 'I don't think either of us will sleep again so after we've finished our tea I'll help you get washed and dressed and then cook our breakfast.'

'I don't need your help.' The words came out more sharply than Karina had intended, but the thought of him attending to her every intimate need was more than she could stomach.

'Very well, if you're sure you can manage.' He tried not to show his hurt but Karina was well aware that he had taken exception to her words, and as soon as he had finished his tea he left the room.

Immediately she got up and went to the bathroom. She had been told not to get her plaster wet so a shower was out of the question, although how she was going to manage without one for six whole weeks she didn't know.

When she was eventually washed and dressed Ford had breakfast almost ready. His hair was still damp from his shower and he wore a clean blue shirt and a friendly smile. Whatever he was feeling was well and truly masked.

'You've managed, then?'

Karina nodded.

'Good. I've laid the table in the dining room so, if you'd like to sit down, I'll bring breakfast in.'

He was being polite but nothing more, and Karina was surprised by how hurt she felt. Nevertheless, she moved through to the other room, feeling clumsy on the unaccustomed crutches, especially as she knew Ford was watching her.

Breakfast was a feast. Freshly squeezed orange juice was followed by bacon, mushrooms and scrambled egg, with toast and marmalade to finish. To her own surprise she ate every scrap, even though she hadn't felt hungry at first. 'That was lovely, Ford,' she said with real appreciation.

'Something you couldn't have quite managed yourself,' he remarked with a smile.

'I guess not,' she said.

'So you're not going to kick me out yet?'

She grimaced wryly and shook her head. 'No, I'm not. I didn't intend to be unappreciative. I'm sorry.'

He shook his head. 'Don't give it another thought. I'm just glad I left some clothes here, that's all. What shall we do with our day? Do you want to stay in or shall we take a trip to the coast?'

'Ford,' she protested, 'you don't have to spend every single hour with me. You must go to work—you can't keep on taking time off.'

'Why not? I'm the boss, I can do what I like.'

'But it doesn't seem right.'

'You worry too much, my sweet. One phone call will do the trick. What is it to be? A day out? Or would you be better off resting that foot?'

Persistence had to be his middle name, thought Karina. She sipped her tea. 'I think I'd like to stay in.'

'Very well, so be it. I shall be your slave for the day. Whatever madam wants madam shall have.'

Karina couldn't help laughing. 'Stop it, Ford, you know I'd never let you be that.'

'I'm serious,' he said. 'Go and sit down somewhere comfortable while I clear this lot away.' When she looked reluctant he said sternly, 'I mean it, Karina.'

The morning passed pleasantly enough. They read the newspapers, played scrabble—Ford winning two out of three games—they had coffee and biscuits at about eleven because they were both hungry after their early breakfast, and for lunch Ford made Spanish omelettes.

Afterwards they both went to sleep on the two separate settees. It wasn't planned. They were both shattered by their sleepless night, and when Karina's eyes began to close Ford made her comfortable and then lay down himself.

For a while he watched her but it wasn't long before he slept too. He dreamt that he and Karina were married and had a family, and that his once-empty house was now filled with laughter and the patter of many feet. When he awoke he wondered whether his dream would ever come true.

Faint heart never won fair lady—wasn't that what they said? Karina was still asleep and he longed to go to her and stroke her rich dark hair back from her face, kiss her, hold her. How his body ached for her.

Many long minutes passed before she finally stirred. Her eyes opened and she looked across and saw him watching her. 'Have I been asleep long?' she asked sleepily.

'A couple of hours.' She looked delightful, with her cheeks flushed and her hair tousled. He'd seen her many times first thing in the morning but never had he felt so drawn to her, so desperate for her. It was all he could do to remain where he was.

'Have you also slept?'

He nodded. 'And I dreamt of you.'

'That's strange,' she said with a smile. 'I dreamt of you as well.'

'What did you dream?' he asked, wondering if he really wanted to know the answer.

'That you asked me to marry you.'

His breath caught in his throat. 'Did you still say no?'

Karina shook her head. 'Actually, I said yes, and we had a wonderful wedding and Charles Forester was the best man and lots of other people I didn't recognise were there as well. I wonder if they're people I know? I wonder if I'm going to get all of my memory back like this—in dreams?'

Her mention of Charles Forester sent a chill down Ford's spine. Some wedding it would be with her one-time lover as best man. He would never allow that. He didn't even want to catch sight of him again. Not ever.

'The mind works in funny ways,' he said. 'I want you to remember things, I truly do, but I don't think it's of paramount importance. What's important is the present. Me and you. What we're going to do with our lives.'

She nodded and said, 'I guess you're right.'

Ford was pleasantly surprised. He wondered what she was trying to say when she sat up and added, 'I know that I'm not always very fair to you, Ford. You deserve better than I give.' She paused, then added, 'I've made a promise to myself that I'm going to be nicer to you in future. I—'

'Karina, you are always nice. I have no complaints.' He couldn't have her putting herself down.

'But I know that you want more than I've been prepared to give,' she insisted.

Ford inclined his head slowly. 'I can't deny that.'

'And so I want you to know that— that I *do* love you, and that—'

'What?' He leapt off his seat and was beside her in two strides. 'Am I hearing correctly?' He knelt at her feet and took her hands into his. 'You *love* me?'

She nodded, looking enchantingly shy and incredibly beautiful.

'When did you…find out?' His heart hammered painfully in his breast. 'Why haven't you told me before?' This was perfection, the answer to his prayers. He couldn't believe it was happening.

'I think I've known since the night we went to see *Buddy*,' she confessed, 'though I've continued to fight it.'

'And you never told me. You wicked, wicked girl.' But he wasn't angry, quite the contrary.

'It doesn't mean that I'm going to marry you tomorrow or anything like that,' she pointed out. 'I have to get used to the idea that I love you first.'

'But it's not out of the question?'

She shook her head.

Ford wanted to leap to his feet and whoop and shout for joy. Instead, he kissed her, a gentle kiss. He was too afraid of ruining these tender new emotions to do any more. Karina loved him! *She loved him!* And one day soon she would be his wife. He had all the patience in the world now.

'My own sweet darling, you have no idea how happy you've made me,' he murmured against her mouth. 'No idea at all. This is something I've hoped and prayed for for so long.'

'I know,' she said quietly, 'and I'm sorry for all the anguish I've caused you.'

'Karina.' He held her face between his palms and looked at her seriously. 'Please don't keep apologising. I'm the happiest man in the world and I'll wait for however long it takes. No, that's not quite true. I can't wait for ever. I need you desperately. But I'll wait a day or two…or a week…or a month.' His words had slowed as he'd watched the expressions on her face. She hadn't been quite so outraged when he'd got to a month.

'I might even wait six weeks,' he added. 'I think I'd

rather like my bride to walk down the aisle without the aid of crutches.'

She smiled then, and of her own volition she hugged him and gave her mouth to him. He felt as though he were soaring a hundred miles above the earth.

He took what was offered, and explored her mouth, tasting, hungering—feeling a thousand electric impulses trigger his body into a scorching mass of energy.

'You really will marry me in six weeks' time?' he asked when he finally stopped for breath. 'I'm not dreaming, am I?'

'It doesn't leave much time for making arrangements,' she said with a wry twist of her lips, lips made soft and red by his very thorough kissing. 'And with my foot like this I can't—'

'Leave everything to me,' he told her autocratically. 'I will send in a dressmaker, a florist, a beautician, a jeweller and anyone else that you might need. You don't have to step out of this room if you don't want to.'

'Ford, you're overwhelming me.'

'Is anything too much for a beautiful lady?' He touched her lips with a gentle finger and when the tip of her tongue came out to moisten it he slid his finger inside her mouth. She sucked it and the feelings that reverberated through him were such that he wanted to make love to her there and then. But he knew he still had to be careful.

'I think,' she said archly, 'that you're afraid that if you have to wait too long I'll change my mind.'

'There's some truth in that,' he agreed.

'I won't,' she said quietly. 'I love you very much, Ford. It's taken me a long time to accept what my feelings are, but they're all the stronger for it. I can't believe that I ever broke off our engagement. I must have been a fool.'

His lips tightened fractionally as he thought about Charles but he had no intention of bringing him into the conversation. Things were finally going his way and he needed to make sure that nothing went wrong.

'Making up has been very much worth it,' he announced with a satisfied smile, 'and I think this momentous occasion calls for a toast. Do you still have that bottle of champagne?' It was one he had bought several months ago—just in case this miracle ever happened.

She nodded. 'It's at the back of the fridge.'

'Already chilled? How very clever of you, my darling.' She looked absolutely radiant. Her eyes were shining and her cheeks flushed. Her lips were still soft from his kisses, simply begging for more. Should he? Or should he fetch the wine? The wine won. He mustn't be too impatient, too greedy, too possessive, because he knew how she'd backed off on several other occasions when passion had got the better of him.

'Don't move a muscle,' he warned her as he left the room. 'This has to be the most wonderful day of my life.'

He found the champagne and the crystal flutes, and when he returned Karina looked as though something magical had happened to her. She was aglow with happiness, more beautiful than he had ever seen her, transformed into a fairy-tale princess. And it was because of him— because she loved him. He had to be the most fortunate man in the world.

'To my beautiful future wife,' he said once the bottle had been opened and their glasses filled. 'To the woman who has given me everything.'

'And to you,' Karina said, touching her glass to his.

'To the man I love with all of my heart. To the most incredibly patient man, to the most thoughtful, to the kindest, to the—'

'Hey, that's enough.' He stopped her with a laugh. 'Don't give me a swollen head. I've done what any man would have done under the same circumstances.'

Karina shook her head. 'Most men would have run a mile. I've been shockingly horrible to you and yet still you continued to care for me and love me. I don't really deserve you.'

'You deserve the best life has to offer, my sweetheart, don't ever forget that. You're the one who's suffered, no one else. It will be an honour and a pleasure to spend the rest of my days making you happy.'

'You do that already,' she said softly.

Ford felt his heart swell with pride and after they had taken sips of their champagne he set their glasses on the table and drew her to him. He held her gently, as though she were a piece of fragile porcelain. She was so precious, this beautiful woman, so very dear to him, and although he wanted desperately to take her to bed he knew that he dared not.

It was all the more pleasing when she reached out and touched his lips, then gently and wonderingly ran her fingers over the planes of his face—her amazing blue eyes watching him closely all the time—pulled his head down to hers and pressed the sweetness of her lips against his.

Was this how a woman felt when she was kissed by a man? he wondered. A feeling that she was burning up inside? A feeling that if it continued it could be relieved only by the physical act of making love?

Well aware that his breathing was growing heavier and that all sorts of satisfied little groans were issuing from his throat, Ford continued to let Karina take the initiative—to touch him, to kiss, to stroke, to incite, almost driving him insane.

'Sweetheart, what are you doing to me?' It was not so much a question as an agonised groan.

'I love you, Ford.'

Her softly spoken words were like music to his ears. 'And I love you, too, my darling, with all my heart, for ever and ever.'

Then it was his turn to kiss her and express the depth of his feelings, to assuage in some small measure the torture she had inflicted upon him. He wanted to become a part of her, to drown in her soul, to make her his in every way possible.

As if in answer to his prayer Karina whispered words he had never expected to hear. 'Ford, make love to me.'

For several seconds he didn't answer. He closed his eyes and held her close, and then he finally breathed, 'If you're sure?'

'Of course, I am. My body is burning up. I can't wait any longer. Don't you feel the same?'

'You bet I do, sweetheart,' he growled. His kisses took on a greater urgency, but it was very slowly and very carefully that he undressed her, kissing every sweet-smelling inch as it was exposed, his passion mounting at the same time. He found it incredibly hard to pace himself when his body so desperately hungered for hers.

He took no time at all to slip out of his own clothes, and then they both lay on the thick cream carpet which cushioned their bodies beautifully and gave them so much more room than a bed would have.

Lord, she was beautiful. It had been so long since he had seen her naked like this, her body ripe for him, al-

ready making instinctive, provocative movements, her
hands seeking and touching and holding—and torturing.
Her lips were parted and moist and offering themselves
to him, her hunger as deep as his own.

There was no time for protracted love-making. They
were both desperate for each other, their breathing
heavy, their hearts and pulses working overtime. When
he touched her she was so ready, so moist, so welcom-
ing, that it took his breath away, and although he wanted
to enter her fiercely, urgently, he forced himself to ease
into her slowly and savour the pleasure.

Karina was shocked to the very core when Ford with-
drew. In a voice almost unrecongisable as his own he
said, 'I can't go through with this, Karina. I'm sorry.'

She stared at him in utter amazement, a sickening,
sinking feeling crawling into her stomach. His face was
so pale she thought he must be ill. 'Ford, what's wrong?'

He shook his head. 'I don't know.'

This confused her even more. 'What do you mean,
you don't know?'

'I just don't know.' He sat back on his heels, his head
in his hands, and she could see that he was trembling.

'Ford, you have to tell me,' she said urgently. This
was weird, unnerving. What had gone wrong? Had he
suddenly found that he didn't fancy her after all? That
he couldn't make love to her? Was she so different? Was
it her fault? Had she done something wrong?

'I can't, Karina. I'm sorry, I can't explain. Look, get
dressed, will you?' He helped her to her feet then, without looking at her, he quickly pulled on his own clothes
and left the room.

Karina burst into tears.

CHAPTER SEVEN

KARINA felt totally humiliated. When she had asked Ford to make love to her it had been a big step, a hard decision—one that she hadn't taken lightly. It had needed a lot of courage.

Why had he stopped at the critical moment? Why had he had second thoughts? She could come up with no logical answer. Had he been afraid of hurting her? Realising that he couldn't wait, that he'd needed to thrust himself urgently into her, had he suddenly been afraid of causing pain since it had been well over twelve months since any man—and she regretfully had to count Charles—had made love to her? But she had been so ready—how could that be?

Certainly some perverse thought had gone through his mind, one that he didn't intend to share with her. Hopefully he only needed time, perhaps just a few minutes to come to terms with whatever had made him withdraw.

The minutes lengthened. She had dressed and was sitting on the settee, waiting, with her arms wrapped around herself, shivering despite the warmth of the day, but no sound came from his bedroom, and she knew that he wouldn't welcome an intrusion from her. This was his problem, something he had to sort out in his own mind, before facing her again.

At least she hoped it was his problem and nothing to do with her. It was just so incredible. She thought back to what had happened, every movement she had made, every word she had spoken, and was sure she had done nothing to put him off.

Half an hour went by before he emerged. She looked at him expectantly, but his eyes blanked her out and he said, 'I'm going out for a while.' She didn't question him.

She was left alone with her troubled thoughts, her embarrassed thoughts. It was unbelievably mortifying to be rejected so unexpectedly, so completely, without a word of explanation. How did he think she felt? Maybe his mind was in torment but didn't he think that she might be equally as disturbed? Perhaps even more so?

Charles once again slipped into her thoughts. Could he be the answer to Ford's behaviour? Ford had said he'd forgiven her, but had this other man come into his mind at the critical moment? Had he realised that he couldn't forgive her after all. It was a heart-rending thought, and surely spelled the end of their relationship.

She made herself a strong cup of coffee to try to clear her mind, but it didn't help. If it hadn't been for her ankle she would have gone out as well. She needed to escape from these four walls, from memories of Ford and his sudden harsh reaction. It would haunt her for ever.

It was late evening before Ford returned. Karina had spent the whole day puzzling over what had happened, driving herself crazy with one thought piling on top of another. She hadn't eaten, simply sipped cup after cup of strong black coffee.

She had put her three solutions into order. Charles was at the top of her list. If Charles wasn't the reason for Ford's odd behaviour then it was because he'd been afraid of hurting her. If it was neither of these it was something she herself had unknowingly done to put him off.

If she'd expected an answer she was mistaken. Ford looked at her oddly and enquired whether he could do anything for her. When she said no he announced that he was going to bed.

'Don't you think we ought to talk?' she asked, knowing that she would spend another sleepless night if she didn't get the matter sorted out.

'There's nothing to talk about,' he answered grimly, looking at her but seeming not to see her. His eyes had a glazed expression.

'I think there is,' she retorted. 'Your behaviour hurts me, Ford. I think I deserve an explanation.'

'I'm sorry if I hurt you,' he intoned flatly.

His response was less than reassuring. 'I don't mean physically,' she declared at once. 'Something shocked you into withdrawing. What was it?'

'I can't tell you, at least not yet.'

Karina shook her head, unable to come to terms with his strange behaviour. 'Was it Charles?'

He frowned, appearing surprised. 'What the hell has Charles to do with it?'

'I don't know,' she answered in some exasperation. 'I've been searching for answers and—'

'You came up with him?' His lips tightened grimly. 'As far as I'm concerned, there is no answer to what happened—unless there's a medical one.' With that cryptic comment he marched into his room and slammed the door—something he'd never done before.

Karina looked after him in amazement. It was stranger and stranger. What did he mean—medical reason? Had he suddenly discovered that he couldn't make love to her? Was that it? Was there something wrong with him?

It was an answer that had simply never occurred to her. All along she'd thought it was her fault. Now she wanted to go after him and question him further, but she knew it would get her nowhere. She would have to wait until morning.

Making her slow, unwieldy way to her own bedroom, Karina was confident that she wouldn't sleep, but no sooner had her head touched the pillow than she was away. She awoke at about six, needing the bathroom, and when she returned to her own bed she found that Ford had brought her a cup of tea.

She hadn't heard him and he hadn't stayed, but the cup sat steaming on her bedside table. She sat on the bed and sipped the hot, sweet liquid, hoping that over breakfast they could talk. Something had to be said, that was for sure. They couldn't go on like this.

However, Ford was still not forthcoming. He kept looking at her with an odd frown as they ate their sausage, tomato and beans. Karina's appetite hadn't returned and she found it difficult to swallow the food, eating hardly anything. Ford didn't do much better.

'Are you ill?' she asked finally when it was clear he wasn't going to say anything. It was such an odd situation. Here she was feeling hurt and worried, and yet at the same time her need for him hadn't gone away. She was so intensely aware of him that it was setting her teeth on edge to try and hide it.

He frowned as he looked at her. 'No, I'm not. Why do you say that?'

Karina shook her head, as if trying to clear her muddled thoughts. 'I thought you mentioned a medical reason for—er—'

'Dammit, Karina, I told you I don't want to discuss it. I think it was a bad idea me staying here after all.'

Her heart dropped like a lead weight and seemed to settle heavily in the pit of her stomach. She looked at him, stunned. 'I hadn't realised it was that bad.' Good Lord, there were things going on here that she knew nothing about—and he wasn't going to tell her! He was leaving her high and dry.

'I'll send in a daily nurse to look after you.'

'That won't be necessary,' Karina told him tersely. Didn't he realise how much he was hurting her? Did he think it had been easy for her to tell him that she loved him—that she wanted him to make love to her? All this time he had been badgering her—and now this! None of it made sense.

'Don't be ridiculous,' he responded crisply. 'You need looking after.'

'Then you stay and do it,' she retorted. 'I don't want anyone else but you.'

He looked stunned, almost appalled, and then all of a sudden there was a loud peal on the doorbell. Someone had got into the building, without using the intercom, had come up in the lift and was outside her door now.

'Expecting someone?' he asked coldly, and Karina knew he was thinking of Charles. Again she felt that her suspicions in believing that Charles was the man who stood between them was right.

'Aren't you going to open it?' Ford wanted to know, still with that hard tone in his voice.

'I'll let you do it,' she said, but she followed him at her much slower pace.

She heard a woman's voice. 'Hello, Ford. I went to your house and you weren't there. I was told I would find you here. What—?'

At the same moment that Karina stared in stunned amazement at what appeared to be her identical image the woman caught sight of her. She stopped talking, her mouth fell open and she took a step forward. 'Ford, please tell me who this is.'

Ford was already looking equally as dumbfounded, and he turned to look at Karina. 'I don't believe this,' he said harshly. 'Someone's having me on.'

'In that case, they're having me on too,' said the newcomer, and she looked crossly at Karina. 'How dare you try to impersonate me? What's your game?'

Karina couldn't speak. She could only stare at this woman who was so astonishingly like her, so much so that they could have been identical twins. What did it mean? Who was she? And why was she accusing her of trying to be someone she wasn't?

When Ford looked at her again with a deep, angry frown it appeared that he was almost as ready to accuse her of being someone else as well. She shook her head. 'I don't know what you mean. I'm me. I'm Karina Philips.'

'No, *I* am Karina Philips,' said the other woman quite loudly and quite firmly. '*You* are an impostor.'

Karina shook her head in disbelief. Everything about this woman was the same. She had the same hair colour in almost the same style, the same build and height, the same cobalt blue eyes, the same pert nose, the same generous mouth. There wasn't one thing that was different. It was chillingly disturbing.

'And you're wearing my clothes,' accused her mirror image icily.

'Ford?' Karina looked at him questioningly, pleadingly. She was unaware that she was trembling, that she could hardly stand and that her crutches were in danger of slipping away from her.

Ford noticed, took a step forward and supported her

elbow, steadying her against him. 'You'd better shut the door,' he said to the woman who had just entered. 'I'm as confused by this as both of you. Perhaps if we sit down and talk we'll somehow find out what's going on.'

He continued to support Karina as they made their way to the sitting room, making sure she was comfortable by placing a footstool to support her leg. She was grateful when he sat down beside her, leaving their visitor to sit opposite them on the other settee.

After a few seconds' awkward silence he said, 'Which one of you is Karina Philips?'

'Me,' they said in unison.

'I mean the *real* Karina Philips,' he directed tersely.

'I am,' they said at the same time.

'Ask me some questions,' said the newcomer peevishly. 'We'll soon find out who's telling the truth. I don't know what this *person* thinks she's playing at—' she spat the word disparagingly '—but I can assure you that *I* am Karina Philips. Always have been, always will be.' She looked directly at Ford as she spoke, and Karina shivered as an icy hand clutched her heart. This woman was so confident, so sure of herself, that maybe she was right. Maybe her own name wasn't Karina Philips after all. How did she know? Ford was the one who had told her who she was.

'OK,' said Ford, looking directly at the outsider. 'Tell me where you were born.'

'According to my father, somewhere in Surrey,' she responded instantly. 'Although we lived in America until I was eight.'

'What are your parents' names?'

'I never knew my mother—she died when I was two. I don't know what her name was. My father rarely spoke about her. His name was Keith. He died thirteen years ago.'

Karina, listening, was appalled to hear that these were the same things that Ford had told her about herself.

'How old are you?' he asked next.

'Twenty-six. Twenty-seven on the third of next month,' she responded confidently. 'Now, let me ask *her* some questions.' She glared at Karina. 'Whereabouts in America did you live?'

'She can't answer that,' Ford said. 'She's lost her memory.'

The woman laughed disparagingly. 'How very convenient. I suppose you can't remember how many schools you went to either?'

Karina shook her head miserably, wishing this woman wouldn't be so horrid to her—that she would talk reasonably and try to get to the bottom of this nightmare.

'Good gracious, Ford, you don't believe that she's me, do you?' questioned the newcomer. 'She's taking advantage of your good nature. She must have known that I'd left you and pretended to be me so that she could live in this sumptuous apartment free. It's clever makeup, I agree, but—'

'It wasn't like that,' said Ford tersely. 'Karina had an accident and spent many weeks in hospital. She didn't know who she was. I brought her back here myself.'

'So how did you know about the accident?' asked the woman.

'A friend of mine actually witnessed it and phoned me.' He seemed confused as he looked at each of them in turn. 'I wasted no time in getting there.'

'But *I* am Karina and I've never had an accident,' insisted the girl who had just walked in and given them both such a shock. 'I can tell you a few details of our love life if you like—I'm sure they will convince you that I am who I say I am.' She gave a sly, mysterious smile as she spoke, and then went on, 'After our engagement ended I went to America to live. I've been there ever since. I came back for a holiday and thought I'd look you up—and this is what I find. An imposter, living in my apartment, pretending to be me.'

There was such a carping edge to her voice that Karina felt obliged to defend herself. 'I was told who I was, and if someone's made a mistake then that's not my fault. But I can understand how it happened. We're so alike it's incredible. We must be related. It couldn't happen otherwise.'

'I have no sisters,' retorted the newcomer.

'I don't know whether I have,' said Karina.

'It's weird.'

'It's unbelievable.'

'I think I need a drink,' said Ford.

It was very early to be drinking but they all had a drink—Ford a whisky and the two girls a gin and tonic—and afterwards they sat, talking and trying to solve the mystery.

Karina was the most disturbed of all. If she was not Karina Philips, who was she? She asked this question time and time again but there was never an answer. Their visitor stayed for lunch and still the conversation centred on their identicalness.

'I can't call you both Karina,' Ford said, when confusion kept arising. 'I think I will choose the initial letter and call you Kay,' he said, looking at her solemnly. To the girl who had just disrupted their lives he said, 'You will be Karina.'

So she was the one who had to change her name, thought Karina unhappily. He had accepted that this other girl was the real Karina. And it would be this girl he loved. Her own unhappiness grew deeper. Everything was getting worse instead of better.

Gradually their visitor became more friendly and interested, asking her all sorts of questions about her accident and what it was like, not being able to remember anything.

But Kay—she had to think of herself as Kay now—had other things on her mind. This identical image of herself was probably the reason Ford had so abruptly stopped making love to her. He'd sensed that she was a different person. Maybe she made love differently, maybe she was shaped differently—something he had discovered only at the last minute.

It tormented her to think that when she had finally, after much deliberation, agreed to marry him it had all so suddenly been snatched away from her. The sad part was that he could never have loved *her*. He had loved the woman he'd thought she was, the woman who was now sitting in the same room. He kept looking at her, and Kay knew that she had lost him for ever. His real love had come back into his life and she had to fade out of it.

When Karina finally said that she had to go because she was meeting someone for dinner Kay did not know whether to be glad or sorry. Ford saw his ex-fiancée to the lift and they talked quietly for several minutes.

He was silent and thoughtful when he came back and Kay—it was difficult to think of herself as that—guessed that he was trying to find the words to tell her to get out. To say that he was sorry he'd made a mistake, but that she was not who he'd thought she was and therefore had no part in his life. She decided to pre-empt him.

'Tomorrow I'll find somewhere else to live,' she told him quietly.

His head jerked and he looked at her as if she were crazy. 'What are you talking about?'

'You won't want me now that the real Karina has come back in your life,' she answered, not realising how miserable she sounded. 'I'm sorry I'm not her. It must be a tremendous shock to you.'

'You're going nowhere,' he told her firmly. 'It's a shock, I allow you, and it was an easy mistake on my part. It's uncanny how alike you two are. But I'm certainly not allowing you to walk out of here. This is your home. It doesn't matter whether you're the Karina I once knew or not. I want you to stay.'

Kay shook her head fiercely. 'It wouldn't be right to take advantage of your generosity any longer.'

'You're talking nonsense, Karina—Kay, I mean. Hell...' He ran agitated fingers through his hair. 'You have to be twins—there's no other explanation.'

'So why were we brought up separately? Why weren't we told about each other?' she wanted to know.

He spread his hands. 'I wish I knew the answer. But someone out there must be desperately worried about you. Maybe we should go to the police and check the missing persons' list.'

'Maybe I should just regain my memory,' she retorted bitterly. He had no idea what it was like to lose even more than she'd had before. To lose her memory had been bad enough, but now she'd lost what little identity he'd given her. She was back to square one. On top of that she had even lost Ford's love. This had to be the worst day of her life.

She was unprepared, therefore, when Ford took her into his arms and held her against the comforting warmth of his body. 'I realise how hard this is for you, my sweet. I wish there was some simple explanation. I wish I could—'

'There's nothing you can do,' she protested, feeling an explosion of heat and desire rush like liquid mercury through her veins, sensitising every one of her nerve endings, setting her on fire. 'This is my problem, mine alone.'

She would love him for the rest of her life. Even though she was sure he could play no part in it she would never forget him. These feelings, which he could arouse so easily, would always be there whenever she thought about him.

'I don't agree,' he said quietly. 'It's my fault you're in this situation. If I'd not scooped you up from the hospital and brought you here you would have probably found your own family by now. Might even have regained your memory. It's no wonder you could remember nothing of what I've told you.'

'How about Charles?' she asked suddenly, pushing herself free of him so that she could see his face properly. 'Tell me about him.'

'It is clear now that Charles Forester has nothing to do with you,' he said gruffly. 'If it makes you feel any better, I feel dreadful for accusing you of having an affair with him.' He tried to take her in his arms again but she resisted.

'But I've dreamt about him,' she contended.

'No, you dreamt about a man named Charles. There are thousands of those in the world.'

'But I also remembered the name, Charles Forester. It's too much of a coincidence for them to be two different people. He must mean something to me. What does he look like?'

'I've never actually met him,' Ford admitted on a deep, reluctant sigh, 'but the friend who saw you—saw Karina—with him described him as being very tall, well over six feet, thin-featured with quite long blond hair brushed back from his face.'

Kay nodded eagerly. 'That's the man in my dream. I must know him, mustn't I? This is astonishing. Can't we find him? Wouldn't he be a clue to my identity?' It was strange that both she and Karina knew this man.

Ford looked as though it was the very last thing he wanted, and she could understand his reluctance, considering that he thought Karina had had an affair with Charles Forrester. Nevertheless, her whole future depended on speaking to this man so surely Ford would help?

'Karina is the only one who knows where Charles lives,' he announced somewhat grimly.

'Then will you ask her next time you see her?'

'You can ask her yourself,' he said. 'I told her I was staying here until your foot's better.'

'So she'll be coming to visit you?' The thought stuck in Kay's throat like a fish-bone. It would be too distressing for words, seeing the two of them together. It would be like looking at herself with Ford, with none of the sensations that normally accompanied such togetherness.

'Not really. She plans to find out whether you two are actually twins. Once she was over the initial shock she was quite excited. She'll be here to tell you her findings.'

Kay would have also been excited if it didn't mean that she was sure to lose Ford. To do so when he was the only person in the world she could relate to, when he was her whole life, made it ten times—no, a hundred times—harder.

However, she said none of this to Ford, asking instead,

'How is she going to manage that if her parents are dead? Does she have other relatives?'

'Not to my knowledge,' Ford answered. 'She's going to make enquiries at the Office for National Statistics.'

Kay felt her heart lurch. It went almost without saying that Karina was her sister but to actually find out for sure would—would what? she wondered. What would it do to her?

If they were twins then who was their birth mother? Karina's mother, who had died? Her own mother, whom she could not yet remember? Or someone different altogether? Had they both been adopted separately? Surely that wouldn't have been allowed? There were so many questions to be answered, so many questions.

CHAPTER EIGHT

KAY'S mind kept whirling in many different directions. She tried to seize every possible explanation, but the more she thought about it the more mystified she became. She was so confused, so tormented, so despairing, that she didn't know which way to turn.

Ford did all he could to comfort her, but she could see that he was also unsettled by this unexpected and illogical turn of events. They talked about it constantly, and to his credit his attitude towards her didn't change one bit. He was still attentive and caring, still held her close, still kissed her, but Kay was sure that he was doing it because he felt sorry for her.

Sometimes he seemed far away and she knew that during those moments he was thinking of Karina, sensuous Karina with the voracious sexual appetite. He was probably regretting what had happened—visiting her in the hospital and bringing her back here. She must have been such a disappointment to him, but he was too much of a gentleman to tell her that. He would let her down very slowly and very gently.

It seemed that their only topic of conversation was centred on Karina, and when two days had passed and they had heard nothing Kay asked, 'Why is it taking her so long?'

'I wish I knew,' said Ford. 'The Statistics Office is in Southport in Merseyside. Maybe she's taking the opportunity to spend a few days in the area.'

Kay thought it odd that Karina hadn't even phoned.

'Are you missing her?' She didn't want Ford to say yes, even though some impulse had demanded she asked the question.

'How can I miss her when I have you?' he asked gently. 'You are the one who means everything to me.' He eased her closer, nestled her in the crook of his arm and stroked back a stray strand of hair from her face.

Kay felt a swift surge of desire, something she had been doing her very best to quell this last couple of days. Such feelings had to be stamped on very thoroughly. They had no part to play in her life any more. He was saying these things to make her happy, but she was sure there was no truth in them. She gave a tiny smile. 'But I'm not who you thought I was. The real Karina is the one out there.'

'Maybe she is,' he murmured, 'but it's you I've nursed through your bad times. You I've asked to marry me. You surely don't think I'm going to leave you high and dry?'

He looked deadly serious but Kay couldn't accept that he meant it. 'You only asked me to marry you because you thought I was the other Karina,' she maintained. 'You don't have to go through with it. I free you from any commitment whatsoever.'

She missed the pained expression that crossed his face, felt only his arm tighten about her. 'And if I don't want that?'

'Of course you want it,' she asserted, while at the same time her heart ran out of control and her pulse throbbed. It was torture to sit so close to him and yet, contrarily, she didn't want to move. Every second they now spent together had to count, had to go into her store of memories for the dark days ahead. She had no doubt in her mind, regardless of what he said, that the day would come when he would choose Karina in preference to herself.

'I think I ought to be the judge of what I want,' he said fiercely, 'and at this moment I want you very much indeed.'

'Enough to want to make love to me?' she asked accusingly.

He knew what she meant. 'I can explain that,' he said, his dark eyes shadowed all of a sudden.

'Can you?' she asked sharply. 'It must be a miracle because you couldn't—or wouldn't—explain before.' He'd hurt her so much that she'd wanted to creep into a corner and die.

'That's because I had no answer.'

Kay didn't believe that for one second. 'It's because she's a better lover than me, isn't it?' she claimed, feeling an acute physical pain at the thought of it.

'No.' He shook his head with great determination. 'It's not that at all.'

'Then what made you reject me at such a crucial moment?' Kay could not keep the hurt out of her eyes or the pain out of her face.

He winced. 'Isn't it clear? You offered me your virginity. Your *virginity*, Kay! When I knew damn well you weren't a virgin. I couldn't understand what was happening when I tried to enter you and— Hell, I was scared. It was something beyond my experience.'

She was a virgin! Kay remembered asking Ford what a virgin was when she'd come across the word in a newspaper. And she was one. It didn't make her feel happy because it proved beyond a shadow of doubt that she wasn't the Karina Philips he'd thought she was. He had made her into this person, never dreaming for one second that the real Karina would turn up. It was an impossible situation. Truly impossible. 'You began to think I was an impostor?' she enquired at length.

'No! Not that. Never,' he answered grimly. 'I actually thought there must be some medical explanation. You had changed in so many different ways that I thought— Oh, I don't know what I thought. I was so mixed up. And I couldn't tell you because...'

'Because what?' she urged.

'Because I didn't know what it would do to you. You've gone through so much these last months, you've been so fragile, that I didn't dare tell you anything that was going to set you back.'

'And you didn't think that spurning me the way you did might have some effect? I was mortified, Ford. I thought I had offended you in some way.'

'Oh, Karina—Kay,' he corrected quickly, 'you could never do that. You are a truly wonderful human being. You would never hurt a soul.'

'Not intentionally,' she admitted, 'but—'

'But nothing, my sweet one. I'm truly relieved that the puzzle has been solved, and I apologise if my actions hurt you.'

He tried to kiss her but Kay turned her head away. One kiss would lead to another, and another, and then what? Much as she loved him and quite desperately wanted him, she couldn't allow him to make love to her. Not now, not when there were two Karinas and his mind was sure to be as mixed up as the coloured pieces of plastic in the kaleidoscope she'd had as a child. *As a child!*

Ford heard her swiftly indrawn breath and he looked at her anxiously. 'What's happened?'

'I just remembered something.'

His breathing stopped too. 'Tell me. Tell me quickly.'

'I had a kaleidoscope when I was a child. You know, one of those—'

'I know what a kaleidoscope is,' he informed her impatiently. 'Go on.'

'That's it, that's all I remember.'

He looked distinctly disappointed. 'I thought it was something of great importance. I thought—'

'It *is* important, don't you realise?' she asked sharply. 'It's another piece in the jigsaw.'

He nodded, though his lips were tight. 'Do you remember anything else about your childhood? Your parents, for example?'

Kay closed her eyes and willed herself to remember. She could see herself, shaking her kaleidoscope and looking at all the marvellous patterns that it made. And she could see the room she was in—a tiny room with a stone floor and a rag rug and well-polished furniture, and little leaded windows through which the sun shone.

'No, nothing except a room,' she said finally. 'And there's no one in it other than me.'

'Try harder,' Ford urged. 'This is a real breakthrough.'

But the effort was giving Kay a headache and she shook her head. 'It's no good, Ford. I can't force memories.'

He grimaced apologetically. 'I know, I'm sorry.'

She wondered whether he really was. He was doing an admirable job of trying to pretend that nothing had changed, but Kay knew that his whole world must have shifted on its axis—as hers had—and it was going to take a long time for either of them to come to terms with it.

They both went to bed that night feeling very sad. Kay wondered as she lay alone in her room whether she ought to have encouraged Ford to make love to her—

maybe stake her claim on him, instead of giving him up to another woman. Except that it was not just any woman. It was very probably her twin sister and in that case she wouldn't want to squabble over him. Karina had first claim on Ford and that was where his loyalties ought to lie. It would be up to Kay to give him up with good grace.

It seemed very strange to think that she probably had a twin sister, especially one who had not known of her existence. She couldn't help but wonder whether she herself had ever been told, whether she'd known she'd had a sister but not her whereabouts. Someone had been cruel and it would undoubtedly leave a deep scar on their psyches for many years to come.

The following morning Ford was his usual concerned self. He enquired how her foot was and made sure she was comfortable as he put her breakfast in front of her. So far neither of them had mentioned Karina. When the doorbell rang they looked at each other. 'Karina!' they said in unison.

Ford answered the door and Kay drew in a deep painful breath as she looked again at her double. It was so weird. It twisted her insides and made her want to shriek out at the unfair trick someone had played on them.

Karina looked intently at her, too, no doubt thinking the same thing.

'Have you eaten?' asked Ford, inviting Karina to sit with them at the table.

'Hours ago,' she answered. 'I was up at the crack of dawn, waiting until I could decently put in an appearance, but I'd love a cup of coffee.'

Ford fetched another cup, poured coffee for her and

then he and Kay looked at her expectantly. 'Well,' he said, 'what did you find out?'

Karina looked at Kay, her blue eyes searching the other's face. 'That we're definitely twins.'

Although they had all known that there could be no other explanation, there was still a stunned silence for a few seconds. Then Kay gave a trembly laugh and Karina looked at her, before pushing her chair back to stand up. Kay did the same, awkwardly because of her plaster cast. The two girls fell into each other's arms, their tears flowing.

It was a union that brought tears even to Ford's eyes, and it was several long minutes before anyone spoke. 'This has to be the most emotional scene I've ever witnessed,' he said gruffly.

'It's unbelievable,' whispered Kay.

'Unreal,' agreed Karina.

'Why weren't we told?'

'Why were we split up?'

There was no answer to either of these questions. 'I was only allowed to look at the index, not the actual birth register,' Karina told them, 'and all it had was our names. But they were there, one after the other, and the woman in charge suggested that I look at my birth certificate because apparently if it's a multiple birth the time is put on it. I didn't have to look because I knew. What I hadn't realised was that it wasn't on everyone's certificate. So if you look on your certificate and—'

'I don't have one,' Kay said quietly. 'It's probably at home, wherever that might be.'

'Oh, Lord, I'd forgotten you can't remember,' Karina said in concern. 'Poor you. You could get a copy, I suppose, but what's the point when you'll find the original as soon as your memory returns? But I did find out one thing,' she added brightly. 'Your name is Kaylee.'

'Kaylee.' Kay said the name experimentally. 'I like it. Yes. Kaylee Philips. It sounds good.' But it didn't bring any more memories back. 'It was an excellent guess on your part, Ford,' she added, 'when you decided to call me Kay.'

'A lucky guess,' he agreed, 'but I'm so pleased that at last you know your identity. Kaylee. A beautiful name for a beautiful lady.'

The girls continued to hold hands as they sat down. They looked constantly at each other, to ask all sorts of questions about their past, none of which Kay could answer and it made her sad. However, she learned a lot about Karina and her father.

'He was a drifter,' Karina confessed. 'We travelled all over America when I was little, and even when we came to England he never stopped in one place for long. He drank a lot as well. It was his undoing, I'm afraid. He died of cirrhosis of the liver when I was thirteen. I was fostered out after that until I was old enough to go it alone.'

Kay hated hearing that her father had been an alcoholic and felt sad that she had never known him. 'And our mother?'

Karina shrugged. 'Father said she died when I was two years old. It was why he went to America. He said he couldn't face the thought of staying where all the memories were.'

'So why didn't he take me as well?' Kay asked sadly, fresh tears coursing down her cheeks. It hurt her terribly to think that her father hadn't wanted her.

'That I can't answer,' replied Karina. 'It's dreadful,

isn't it? I guess we'll never know. But at least we have each other now.'

Kay nodded and squeezed Karina's hand. 'I wonder what happened to me. Whether I was fostered or adopted.'

'You'll find out one day,' Karina told her confidently. 'And I truly hope that they are happy memories.' They got up and hugged each other again. Then Ford took his turn. Kay didn't want to feel jealous when he kissed Karina, but she did. She was sure that she would have to give him up but it would be hard, so very, very hard—made even more difficult because she would be forced to see the two of them together for the rest of her life if they did finally get married.

They sat and talked, Kay asking eager question after eager question until finally she asked the one which had been on the tip of her tongue all morning. 'I was wondering, Karina, whether you could tell me where Charles Forester lives.'

She felt Ford stiffen at her side. This was the man who had caused the split between him and Karina. He was a man Ford hated with every fibre of his being, but he also knew how important it was to Kay that she located Charles.

'Charles Forester?' Karina looked from Kay to Ford and back again to her sister. 'Is this some kind of joke? Has Ford put you up to this?'

Kay shook her head vigorously. 'Of course not, but it's very important to me. I think he might hold a clue to my past life.'

'You do?' enquired Karina, frowning now and spoiling the smooth perfection of her brow. 'Why? How?'

'I think he's someone I once knew.'

'*You* knew him?'

'That's right,' agreed Kay. 'I've dreamt about him. I even saw him a few days ago, but he disappeared before I could catch up with him.'

There was a gasp from Ford. 'You never told me that.'

'I know,' she admitted with a wry grimace. 'At the time you were exhibiting very jealous tendencies as far as he was concerned, and I didn't think you'd want to hear.'

'He accused *me* of having an affair with him,' Karina put in quietly.

Kay nodded. 'He mentioned it when he thought I was you.'

'So you got the brunt of his anger as well?'

'Not exactly,' said Kay with a smile, 'although I do seem to remember him telling me that I'd had a *convenient* memory lapse.'

Ford grumbled something deep within his chest and the two girls laughed.

'As for me knowing Charles,' said Karina, 'it's simply not true. I'd never even heard of him until Ford brought him up. But would he listen? No. I got so rattled I could have choked him. And I knew I couldn't marry a man who didn't trust me...'

'So you threw your ring back at him,' Kay finished with a laugh.

Karina nodded. 'Wouldn't you have done the same?'

Before she could answer Ford said, 'So, if it wasn't you, Karina, it must have been Kay whom Geoffrey saw with Charles Forester.'

'If he *was* my friend,' Kay said, 'and as close as you suggest he was, why didn't he come to see me in hospital?' At least she now knew that they had never been lovers. The thought had always been abhorrent to her, and it had pleased her immensely when she'd discovered that she was a virgin.

'It could be that he never found out,' suggested Ford.

'Some friend, then,' she said scornfully. 'But I need him now. The question is, though, how can I find him if none of us knows where he lives?'

'Try the phone book,' suggested Karina, and while Kay limped off to fetch it she said to Ford, 'I think, Ford Fielding, that you owe me an apology.'

He inclined his head gravely and moved to sit at her side. 'Indeed I do. It was very wrong of me to jump to conclusions, without listening to what you had to say. I apologise most profusely. I am deeply sorry.'

Karina's stern frown dissolved into a smile. 'Kiss and make up?'

He nodded and leaned forward to kiss her briefly, but Karina had other ideas and hooked her arms around his neck and kissed him properly, her lips full on his. 'Hold me, Ford,' she muttered. 'It's been so long. I want to make sure that—'

They both heard the sound at the same time—the crash of the telephone book to the floor as it slipped out of Kay's nerveless fingers. She had used only one crutch so that she could carry the book, and that now fell to the floor too.

Kay hadn't expected Ford to home in on Karina quite so quickly. She'd thought he would at least wait until he got her on her own. Kay wanted to pick up the book and sling it at them, and would have done so had she not found it ungainly on her one good leg.

But, damn, did they have to do it in front of her? Didn't they realise how it would make her feel? Hot tears stung her eyes and she blinked them back with strong determination. 'Sorry,' she said brightly.

'Here, let me help you.' Ford sprang to his feet and
helped her back to her seat, putting the telephone directory on her lap. 'I apologise, I should have fetched it for
you. I should have known that—'

'For heavens' sake, Ford, don't fuss,' she snapped.
'Haven't you ever dropped anything?'

He looked shocked by her sharp words. 'I guess I
have. I'm sorry, I was just trying to help.'

'I don't need your help.' She opened the directory,
found the Fs and concentrated all her attention on looking for Charles Forester. Neither of them knew that she
couldn't see a thing. Tears were blurring her vision and
she was afraid that they might fall onto the pages and
give her away.

Ford sat bedside her and she wanted to yell at him to
go way and rejoin his love on the other side of the room.
She felt sickened at the thought that they hadn't been
able to wait a second. How long did they think it took
to fetch a phone book out of the hall? Hadn't either of
them cared that she might see them in each other's arms?

She couldn't blame Karina but Ford should have
known it would hurt her, even though she had told him
that he could consider himself a free man. If he'd had
any feelings at all for her he would have waited until
he'd got Karina on her own. It was an insult, one that
would stick with her for a long, long time.

'Have you found his number?' It was Karina enquiring, showing no sign at all that she was embarrassed by
the situation.

'Not yet,' Kay managed, and with grim determination
she blinked back her tears and made herself focus on the
names and numbers. But there was no Charles Forester
listed, which was a bitter disappointment. She slammed
the book shut. 'Nothing.'

'Are you sure?' asked Ford.

'Absolutely. Look for yourself if you don't believe me,' she said irritably.

'No, no,' he said at once, looking surprised by her sudden outburst. 'I believe you, of course I do. It means he either doesn't live in this area or he's ex-directory. There must be some way of finding him, though. Why don't we discuss it over lunch? I think we should all go out to celebrate you two finding each other.'

Karina immediately shook her head. 'Sorry, I can't,' she admitted ruefully. 'I'm expecting a phone call and need to be back in my hotel.'

'In that case,' Ford said, 'Kay and I will have to celebrate alone. Unless you're free tonight?'

Again Karina shook her head. 'I have other plans. I'm busy, catching up with all my old friends. I can make it tomorrow, though.'

Ford smiled his pleasure. 'Tomorrow it is, then. Do you mind waiting another day, Kay?'

She shook her head, not trusting herself to speak. She liked the idea of celebrating but would have preferred to do it with Karina alone. She didn't want to witness the two of them together, see the sparks of attraction run from one to the other. It was there already—she was sure, she could sense it, feel it, almost taste it.

The love Ford had felt and shown for herself had really been directed at Karina. It was only right, she thought, that he should now transfer his love back to the woman he had fallen in love with in the first place.

If he hadn't loved Karina he would never have raced to the hospital when he'd heard about the accident. He would never have spent so much time tending to her every need. And he would never have kissed Karina so ferociously the moment her own back was turned.

'How long are you over for?' she heard Ford ask.

'I'd planned on a month originally,' Karina answered, 'but I hadn't realised how much I'd missed England.' She looked purposefully at Ford as she spoke, confirming in Kay's eyes that it was Ford she'd missed more than the country. An even deeper sadness enveloped her. There had been a vain hope at the back of her mind that Karina might not love Ford any more.

'So you might not go back—is that what you're saying?' he queried, and Kay thought he looked pleased.

'Not exactly,' Karina informed him. 'I might stay a bit longer, though. I do have a job out there, don't forget.' She had already told them that working as a graphic designer for a big advertising agency was paying her oodles more money than she'd ever earned in England.

It made Kay wonder what her own chosen career had been. Did she have a job or had she been one of the unemployed? If she had worked, what had they thought when she never turned up again? There were so many unanswered questions—so many things that she had to readjust to—that her mind spun out of control.

'You might earn good money but it must be costing you a small fortune in that hotel you're staying in,' Ford told Karina. 'My house is sitting empty. If you want to stay there please feel free.'

Kay felt as though he'd stabbed her in the back. Conversely, Karina beamed her pleasure. 'What a wonderful idea. I might take you up on that.'

'You'll be very welcome,' he said. 'My staff will be delighted to have someone to look after. I seem to have spent more time here lately than at home.'

Was that criticism she heard in his voice? Kay's heart gave a further lurch. There seemed no end to her torment.

'You mean you won't be there?' Karina looked and sounded disappointed.

Kay swallowed her hurt and said quickly, 'Of course he'll be there. I don't really need you, Ford. I can manage perfectly well on my own. Goodness, it's been so long since you and Karina last saw each other that there must be loads for you to catch up on. Go back home, please. I'd rather you did.'

He shook his head. 'I couldn't do that to you, and I don't think Karina would expect it. Of course I'll spend some time with Karina, but you're not going to get rid of me that easily.' He tried to make a joke of it, but Kay was sure that it was only his conscience that forced him to say these things. No man in his right mind would tie himself to an invalid when he could spend time with the woman he loved.

'I'll leave you two to sort things out,' said Karina with a light laugh. 'Will you pick me up tomorrow, Ford?'

'Naturally,' he said softly, looking at her in a way that left Kay in no doubt as to his feelings. It was the way he'd looked at her when he'd thought she was Karina. What a farce. It should have been a pleasure to discover that she had a twin—instead, it was causing heartache. Would she ever manage to bury her love sufficiently to look kindly on her sister and Ford?

Karina hugged Kay once more before she left. Ford opened the door for her and walked over to the lift to press the button, wondering as he did so what he had done wrong in this life for fate to thrust him into such a tricky situation. How could fate be so cruel? He had no doubt in his mind which one of the twins he was in love with, but it was not that simple. One of them was going to end up hurt.

'I wish I could have made it today,' said Karina apologetically. 'It's incredible, isn't it, finding I have a twin sister?'

He nodded. 'It's mind-blowing.'

'I hope Kay and I are going to be good friends. I hope we get on.'

Ford frowned. 'Is there any reason why you shouldn't?'

'Only you,' said Karina softly. 'We both love the same man, don't we? The problem is—which one of us do *you* love?'

Kay was busy loading their breakfast dishes into the dishwasher when Ford returned. 'You shouldn't be doing that,' he told her reprovingly.

'I'm trying to convince you that I can manage,' she retorted, wishing he wouldn't fuss so. 'I'm not completely disabled, you know. I can look after myself.'

'You know very well that you don't have to prove anything to me.' He came up behind her and slid his arms around her waist, pulling her back against him.

She felt the hardening of his body, his swift arousal, and her own body felt supercharged in response. But she wished he hadn't done it. She would rather he admitted right now that he had made a mistake and that it was Karina he loved. Holding her like this, which suggested that nothing had changed, wasn't going to make things any easier.

'Don't, Ford.' She turned away from him before she gave way to the bone-melting sensations that were skipping far too rapidly through her limbs. 'I don't want you to touch me.'

'Why the hell not?' He growled his displeasure. 'You're surely not still of the opinion that my loyalties lie with Karina?'

'Of course they do,' she told him firmly, 'but that's

not the reason.' She had to lie for the sake of her tormented mind. 'I feel peculiar, that's all.'

A frown tugged at his brows. 'You mean you're ill?'

'No.' Kay shook her head. 'I'm not sick, not in that way. It's the situation. I haven't known for the last twelve months whether I have any family or not, and to discover that I have a twin, whom I wouldn't have known about anyway, is really very scary.'

Ford nodded sympathetically. 'It's an awful deed someone has done—splitting the two of you up. You've missed the best years of your lives.'

'I know. I keep thinking about it, and it's even more important now that I get my memory back. There's so much I need to know, to find out. Maybe we should go to the police after all and see if I've been registered as missing.'

'*I'll* do it,' said Ford. 'I'll make us some lunch and then go.'

'I'm not hungry,' said Kay at once. 'I'd rather we found out now. I don't want to waste another minute. I'm coming with you.'

They drew a blank. There were no records anywhere of a Kaylee Philips being reported missing, and when they returned to the apartment Kaylee was close to tears.

Ford turned her into his arms. 'There's still Charles Forester, my darling. I reckon he's your best hope.'

'My last hope,' she declared firmly. 'But how am I going to find him? It was a thousand to one chance I saw him the other day. I can't hang around on street corners just in case.'

'It is a problem,' he agreed, 'but it's one we'll sort out together. Don't worry about it.'

He was making it sound as though they were still a couple, and when he tilted her chin with a gentle finger

and he lowered his mouth to hers Kay knew that she
ought to push him away, that this wasn't the answer to
her problem.

But somehow sensations pervaded her, making it impossible to move. She was aware only of the sizzling
desire which shot through her veins with alarming speed,
aware of a hunger so deep that she didn't want to deny
it. It was wrong, and she would regret it afterwards, but
at this moment she needed Ford, needed him badly—
needed his comfort, his kisses and whatever else he had
to offer.

CHAPTER NINE

'TO KAY and Karina. To the coming together of the most beautiful twins in the whole world. May you spend the rest of your lives finding true happiness with each other.' Ford proposed the toast and the two girls smiled as they raised their glasses.

Karina was, indeed, looking supremely happy but Kay, beneath her smile, was deeply disturbed because— as well as the unsettling discovery that she was not who she'd thought she was—she'd had another dream last night about Charles Forester, and it troubled her immensely.

The dreams must be trying to tell her something, but what? Ought she to consult someone—find out what they were all about? They were such wildly erotic dreams. In them there was nothing they did not do together. Considering she was a virgin, how did she even know about some of the things they practised?

She went hot at the very thought, and Ford looked at her in concern. 'Are you all right, Kay? You look very flushed all of a sudden. You're not ill, are you?'

'Of course not,' she demurred fiercely. She hadn't told Ford that she had dreamt about Charles again in case he asked what the dream was about. It would have been profoundly embarrassing to discuss such intimate matters.

Both times before when she'd had such dreams she had, on waking, pretended it had been Ford who'd been making such exquisite love to her. She'd actually revelled in her exciting, exhilarating thoughts, but not to-day. Ford no longer belonged to her, she thought. She no longer had any right over his body—and that meant her thoughts about him had to be curtailed as well.

The fact that he'd kissed her so thoroughly last night, and she'd responded wholeheartedly, she refused to ac-knowledge. She'd treated it as one last right before he left her altogether.

It had almost ended with them going to bed together. Only by the sheer force of mind over matter had she managed to walk away from his embrace and his kisses, which had threatened to drown her in a tide of emotion.

It had begun with a kiss so sweet that she'd tingled right to the tips of her fingers and toes, feeling as though an electric current was running through her. The current had become stronger as his tongue had stroked her lips and entwined with hers.

All thoughts of Karina had been forgotten as she had knotted her fingers in his hair and held his head close, taking everything that he had to offer and adding some of her own.

Her body had urged itself closer, wanting to feel every pulsing male inch of him. Her nerves had vibrated with desire, her heartbeat accelerated out of control and a trembling threatened her limbs.

'I don't think you have any idea what you do to me,' he muttered throatily. 'It's impossible for me to keep my hands off you.' Even as he spoke his hands moved from her waist to cup her taut breasts, and when his thumbs stroked her already pert nipples rivers of ecstasy poured through every vein.

Kay knew she ought to stop him, ought to move, ought to protest. She knew she would be furious with herself afterwards, but a consuming need enveloped her.

Her body responded with heated fervency to his kisses, to his touch, to the erotic male smell of him. It was fired with a passion so intense that she couldn't stop herself leaning into him.

The hardness of his arousal scorched through the thin material of her skirt, and brought her halfway back to her senses. This was insanity, the very last thing she should be doing. A few more minutes and all would be lost. And to what avail? He would still leave her. He still belonged to Karina. What was she thinking, allowing him to kiss her so possessively, so wantonly, so *absolutely beautifully*?

'I'm sorry, Ford.' She pushed him away desperately. 'I must be out of my mind. You can't do this any more. You belong to Karina.'

Pain darkened his eyes. 'Kay, my sweet, do you think I would turn my back on you after what we've been through together?'

'I don't care what we've been through,' she cried, but in truth she cared very much. She had bonded with Ford far more deeply than she'd ever imagined possible, and it was going to break her heart to give him up. She could only hope and pray for her memory to return, perhaps to find that she already had a boyfriend and that she could walk out on Ford without any more of this heartache.

'I think you're lying,' he said, 'but I'll yield to your pressure—for the time being.'

'You look miles away,' Karina's voice broke into her thoughts.

'I'm trying to get used to the fact that I have a twin,' Kay managed with a wry smile.

Karina nodded. 'I agree, it's a staggering discovery. I've thought of nothing else myself. When my friend phoned from Seattle I told him about it and he was shocked.'

A male friend, thought Kay. Did that mean…? No. If Karina had a boyfriend she wouldn't have made her preference for Ford quite so clear. Even today, when they'd picked her up at the hotel, she'd kissed Ford with a blatant disregard for Kay, watching. It had been a long, warm, sensual kiss, which had set Kay's teeth on edge. She'd had to turn away.

Now, in Rule's restaurant, in this most exquisite establishment where the dignified service was unparalleled, Karina was still focussing her attention on Ford. Her hand touched his arm often as she spoke and her eyes were constantly on his. He, in turn, paid her far more attention than he did Kay.

She was surprised that he'd noticed the swift colour now flooding her face. She hadn't seen him looking at her. She'd been so deeply involved with her thoughts that he could have made love to Karina on the restaurant floor and she wouldn't have noticed.

But she was the full focus of his attention now—and it was disconcerting. He was very adept at reading her mind and she didn't want him to know her thoughts.

'We were just discussing me going to live in Ford's house,' said Karina, apparently unaware of their tension.

Kay grasped the subject eagerly. 'I think it's an excellent idea.' To Ford she added, 'You'll be moving back there, of course?'

He looked guilty when he said, 'I've decided to share myself between you. I can't leave you, Kay, to fend for yourself entirely, but I do feel I should spend time with Karina.'

Because I'm sure you're still in love with her, added Kay silently and bitterly. And because he was a gentle-

man to the tips of his toes he didn't want to let Kay
down either. He felt he owed her something.

The truth was he owed her nothing—and she owed
him a great deal. He had given up twelve months of his
life because of her and had spent heaven knew how
much money on her. He simply didn't need to do another
thing. Damn him, why couldn't he accept that? It would
make things easier all round if he returned to Karina and
washed his hands of her.

Or would it?

She was living in a void and without Ford she would
probably go to pieces—and he knew it. He probably felt
sorry for her and thought that if he could keep up the
pretence of loving her then Kay would eventually pull
through it. But would Karina allow that?

One only had to look at her to see that Karina was
brimming over with love for Ford. It was there in her
sparkling eyes, in her cheeks which held the glow a
woman in love had. It was there for the world to see.

'Ford,' Kay said impatiently, 'I've already told you
that I don't need you. You needn't spend any time at all
with me. If I had some money, if I had a job and was
earning, you wouldn't see me for dust. I'd be out of here
like a shot.'

'On your crutches?' he enquired with a grin.

'You know what I mean,' she muttered unhappily.

'Don't tease her,' said Karina. 'She has my deepest
sympathy. I'd be as prickly as a porcupine if I had to
put up with half Kay's problems. And if Kay doesn't
mind you spending time with me then you shouldn't try
to dissuade her.'

Kay had the feeling that Karina wasn't being quite
sincere—that she was thinking only of herself. They

might look alike, they might seem identical on the surface, but that was as far as it went.

Whereas Kay was prepared to give Ford up because his first love had returned to the scene, Karina would probably never do any such thing—would never even think about it. She wanted Ford and she intended to have him, whether she was hurting her sister or not.

After lunch Ford took Kay back to the apartment, before announcing that he was going to help Karina move her stuff into his Hampstead home. 'Are you sure you'll be all right?' he added anxiously.

Did she have any choice? Kay asked herself. Any at all? She put on a brave face. 'Ford, if you say that again I'll slosh you one. Of course I'll be all right.'

Karina gave her twin a quick hug. 'Come on, then, Ford. I can't wait to move into your wonderful mansion. I always loved it. I used to visualise myself being mistress there.'

Kay felt a sharp stab of pain and when Ford attempted to kiss her she pushed him away abruptly, forcing a laugh. 'No time for that. Karina is eager to get going. And I don't blame her. Moving in with you has to be a thousand times better than living in a hotel.'

He looked reluctant as Karina tugged him towards the door, and gave Kay one last final, rueful smile as he closed it behind him.

Kay collapsed onto a chair but she refused to let the tears fall. She had to be strong. She had to deal with the situation sensibly. Her love was something that had developed gradually, at Ford's insistence, and it was something that she now had to undo. If that were possible.

She needed to get herself a job. She needed something that would take her out of this apartment for a major part of each day, fill her mind and blank out all thoughts of Ford. As soon as she was earning and she had money she'd move into a smaller, cheaper place, and cut Ford out of her life altogether.

That won't be possible, claimed her inner voice. You're forgetting Karina. She's a part of your life now and if she and Ford get married then he will be part of your life as well. It was a chastening thought.

She could move away, though. She didn't have to live anywhere near them. Surely she could handle seeing them together occasionally?

Had she been brought up with her twin, Kay felt sure she wouldn't want to be parted from her. They would have been so close that they'd live virtually in each other's pockets. But as she'd only met her three times there were no such ties yet.

It was Ford who stood between them, Ford who would be the making or breaking of their relationship, and it was sad to think that she and Karina might never be really close because of their love for this dangerously attractive man.

Even thinking about Ford brought a treacherous weakness to her limbs, a fluttering in her stomach, a real need to be with him—to be held by him, kissed, touched, made love to.

She crossed her arms over her chest and rocked backwards and forwards until the feelings subsided and she was able to think rationally again.

It was then that Kay decided to go out. To sit and think about the two of them together was doing her no good at all.

She cursed her plaster cast, which made it so awkward to walk, but she had become quite adept on the crutches, and she let herself out of the flat and went down in the lift. She walked all the way into Richmond, instead of taking a bus, which was something of a feat but she managed it. Once there she was swept up with the vibrancy of life around her.

A kind young man took pity on her when the traffic wouldn't stop and helped her across the road. She took coffee in one of the small cheerful cafés, bought a book she had been promising herself for ages and a jumper from the new autumn collection.

Just as she was debating whether to return to the apartment or go to the cinema she felt a hand touch her shoulder.

'It is you, isn't it?'

It was a man's voice, not one she recognised, and she was in no position to swivel quickly and look at him.

'I don't recall the crutches but I'd know that hair anywhere.'

Kay had pulled her hair out of its restraining band and let it flow freely down her back before she'd left the apartment. But she wasn't thinking about her hair—she was trying to cope with the fact that there was someone standing behind her who knew her.

Her heartbeats accelerated and her pulses pounded. Someone from her past? Was she going to learn the truth at last? Or was he mistaking her for Karina?

The man moved into her line of vision. The man of her dreams! The man she had seen the other day. Narrow-faced, swept-back blond hair, tall, very tall, handsome, expensively dressed. Yes, one and the same person.

'Kaylee, you're looking at me as though you've seen a ghost,' he remarked drolly.

'Are you Charles Forester?' she asked in a hoarse whisper. This was totally unbelievable and yet it was the answer to her prayers.

His lips twisted wryly. 'Of course I'm Charles. How could you ever forget me. I thought you'd gone to work abroad? What happened?' He looked questioningly at her injured foot.

'Forget that,' she said quickly and dismissively. 'You have no idea how pleased I am to see you, none at all. We need to talk. Now. Are you too busy?'

He continued to look amused. 'I guess I could spare you an hour or so. I was on my way home but there's no rush. I wasn't looking forward to an evening alone. Where do you suggest we go? A meal somewhere perhaps? We could talk over that.'

Kay shook her head firmly. 'I'd prefer it if you came to my apartment. I don't want any diversions.'

'Goodness, Kaylee, I don't get many offers like this.' He smiled broadly, revealing slightly uneven white teeth. He had a tiny, neat moustache as well and he wore a very flamboyant aftershave.

Kay's eyes flashed. 'I'm not offering you anything.' However, her body grew warm as she recalled her erotic dreams where there had been no holds barred between herself and this man. It sent the blood racing frantically through her veins and she was glad he couldn't see inside her head.

'Don't worry, Kaylee, I'm teasing. You never did let me get too close, even though I tried my very best.'

They took a taxi. Charles solicitously helped her in, containing his curiosity during the short journey and telling her instead about the difficult day he'd had. Kay gathered that he was some big noise in a financial institution in the City, and because the stock market was very fragile at the moment they had been inundated with calls from worried clients.

'It brightened up my day when I saw you,' he declared. 'I must have told you this before, but I never imagined that you would grow into such a ravishingly beautiful lady. You were such a skinny child with braces on your teeth, which I used to tease you about mercilessly, much to your fury and embarrassment.'

'You knew me when I was child?' she asked, her heart skipping a beat. This was more than she had expected.

'Of course I knew you, you funny thing. What is this? What's going on?'

'I'll tell you in a minute,' Kay said as the taxi drew up to the kerb. She wanted to pay but Charles insisted. He looked contemplatively at the luxurious apartment block and once inside he gave a whistle of admiration. 'You've done all right for yourself.'

'It doesn't belong to me,' Kay said with a shake of her head.

'Ah.'

'And it's not what you think,' she admonished. 'Come and sit down. There is so much I want to know.'

Once inside the apartment he sat beside her on the settee. Kay turned to him and said, 'I've lost my memory, Charles. I had an accident and since then—nothing, just nothing.'

His grey eyes widened. 'Is that so? How incredible. How intriguing. But...' he frowned, perplexed '...you knew me?'

'I know. One or two things have flashed into my mind recently. Your face is one of them.' She daren't tell him about the dreams. 'So are a room in some sort of stately building and one in a tiny cottage.'

Charles nodded.

'You know them?' she asked eagerly.

'I know them very well. The stately building is my family home in Staffordshire. I go back there occasionally, although my wife and I live here in Richmond for most of the year. The cottage is where you used to live in the grounds of the estate. Your mother worked for my parents. She was head cook.'

Kay clapped her hands in ecstasy. 'Oh, Charles, you don't know what this means to me. I've lived for months with no past. It's been a nightmare. You must tell me where it is. I must go there. I must find my mother and explain what has happened.'

Except that it wouldn't be her real mother, would it— not the woman who had given birth to her? It would be someone she'd called mother, someone who'd brought her up as her own and very probably adopted her—but had never told her the truth! How that thought hurt. But not so much as the thought that her father hadn't wanted her at all.

He'd abandoned her when their mother died and he'd taken only Karina to America. How could he have done that? How had he decided which twin to take? It was sad to realise that she would never find out, but maybe it was as well because she would have hated him intensely.

'I'm sorry, Kaylee,' Charles was saying, 'but your mother doesn't live there any longer. She moved out several years ago. I have no idea where she is now.'

Kay stared at him in frustration but she was determined not to let it faze her. Perhaps the very act of returning to where she had spent her childhood would trigger her memory. If not, someone had to know where her mother had gone. It was a matter of finding and asking the right person.

They talked and talked, Kay asking him all sorts of questions about her past life. He knew very little, except that she had been someone to tease when he came home from boarding school during the holidays. He was an only child and she'd been the only other child on the estate, but because he was five years older—and because she was a girl—he had been very condescending towards her.

'Then, when we bumped into each other last year,' he went on, 'I couldn't believe what a beautiful woman you had grown into. Make no mistake about it, Kaylee, I wanted you. You stirred my blood like no one had in a long time. I wanted to take you to bed—and I might have done if I hadn't confessed that I was married. You have admirable principles. Such a pity.' He shook his head sadly but he was smiling nevertheless.

'So, what was I doing in London? You said something about me going abroad?'

'That's right. You had this self-righteous idea about doing good in some Third World country. I can't remember exactly where you said you were going, but you were spending a week in London first because you'd never been there and so I honoured you, by squiring you around. It didn't get me anywhere,' he added with a rueful grimace. 'The last time I saw you was the day before your flight.'

That accounted for the fact that he had never been to see her in hospital. He had simply never known that she was still in England.

She told him about her accident, about Ford thinking she was Karina and the shock they had both felt when her twin sister had turned up.

'There was definitely only one of you on the family estate,' he said firmly. 'Lord, I'd have had a field day with two of you to torment.' On a quieter note he said, 'Your mother—your adoptive mother, I presume—was a very reserved woman. I used to creep downstairs sometimes and listen to the servants but your mother never joined in the gossip. I don't think anyone knew very much about her.'

'Did she have a husband?'

Charles shook his head. 'I understood she was a divorcée.'

'Oh!' Kay digested this piece of information. It must have happened after she herself had been adopted. Hadn't her step-father liked her? Had she been the cause of their problems? It was all very unsatisfactory and unsettling, and the sooner she found out the truth of the situation the better she would like it.

It was almost midnight before Charles declared he ought to go. Time had gone so quickly that neither of them had realised how late it was. She'd made sandwiches and they'd drunk coffee and wine, but almost without noticing as there had been so much they'd had to talk about.

'You're the best thing that's happened to me,' she declared fervently, standing with him just inside the main entrance door to the apartment.

'Better even than discovering you have a twin sister?' he asked with raised eyebrows.

'That's different,' she said. 'The important thing is that I've found out who I am.'

'If you like,' said Charles, 'I could take you to Staffordshire this weekend. Show you around the Hall and where you used to live—see if it jolts any memories.'

'I think I'd like that,' said Kay, smiling eagerly. 'Can't you make it tomorrow?' It was Wednesday now and she didn't want to wait.

'No can do, I'm afraid,' he said ruefully. 'Pressure of

business, you understand. But I'll pick you up on Saturday morning, say, about eight.'

'Couldn't we go earlier?' she wanted to know.

He laughed. 'Whatever time you like. Seven? Six?'

'Six-thirty,' Kay declared. 'I'll be ready and waiting. Thank you, Charles, for being a life-saver.' She stood on tiptoe—difficult with one foot in plaster and balanced on crutches—and kissed him warmly on the cheek, then nearly fell over as both of her crutches slid to the floor.

His arms saved her, strong powerful arms that wrapped themselves around her—and Ford chose that moment to quietly unlock the door and push it open. His shocked eyes took in the scene at a glance, and without a word he turned again and left, catching the lift before it went back down.

'Oops,' said Charles.

'Damn,' said Kay.

'Ford, I presume? Was he being diplomatic? Or was jealousy his motive for retreating so abruptly?'

As she hadn't told Charles that she was in love with Ford, or that he had asked her to marry him before Karina had turned up again, she looked at him in some surprise. 'I would think diplomacy,' she lied.

He nodded. 'If you say so.' But it seemed to Karina that he didn't believe her. Was she really so transparent? Had she made her feelings known as she'd spoken about Ford and all that he had done for her?

'Shall I chase after him and explain? I'm sure he'll be delighted when he finds out why I'm here.'

Kay shook her head. 'I'll tell him when I see him.' When that would be was anyone's guess because he was probably making his way swiftly back to Karina right now, very likely into her bed. Lord, how the thought hurt.

'In that case,' Charles said, 'I'll bid you goodnight. I'll see you on Saturday bright and early.'

He hadn't been gone five minutes when Ford burst back in. She'd just finished taking off her make-up and brushing her teeth, though she hadn't yet changed into her nightdress.

'What the hell's going on,?' he demanded of her, his eyes stormy and accusing, his face all harsh lines and angles. 'That was Charles Forester, wasn't it? What were you doing in his arms?' His lips curled in distaste.

'As a matter of fact,' she said haughtily, angry with him because he had jumped to conclusions and understanding now why her sister had finished their engagement, 'I was thanking him for telling me who I am and where I live. So it might please you to know that on Saturday he's taking me to meet my family. I won't be a burden to you any longer.'

CHAPTER TEN

'THERE is still lots I don't know,' admitted Kay, 'but it's a beginning, a real breakthrough as far as I'm concerned. I'm so excited.' Ford's initial anger and suspicion had soon dissipated when they began to talk and she told him what had happened.

It still came as a surprise, though, when he suddenly said, 'What's going to happen now with you and Charles?'

It should have been the last thing on his mind. Wasn't he happy for her? Wasn't he interested in finding out about her lost life? Wasn't he overjoyed? What had she and Charles got to do with anything? It sounded as though he was really jealous yet she knew that couldn't possibly be the case.

'You're forgetting he's married,' she said. 'Nothing is going to happen because nothing ever happened before.'

'And I'm supposed to believe that, am I? He tells you how beautiful you are, that the ugly duckling has turned into a swan—but nothing happened!'

'You know darn well it didn't,' she snapped. 'He was just company for the week I was spending in London.'

Kay wanted to say more, but realised the futility of it. Nothing would change Ford's attitude. She deliberately moved on. 'I suppose the fact that I was going to work abroad for twelve months explains why I was never listed as a missing person. I probably also told my mother that it would be difficult to get messages back.'

Ford nodded his understanding. 'She must still be

worried, though. You'd have been back home by now, surely?'

'That's why I must try to find her,' she said urgently.

'I could take you,' he offered. 'You needn't wait until Saturday.'

She liked the idea very much but it wasn't an option. 'I don't know where to go.' Her tone was sorrowful, apologetic. 'I need Charles. He's the only person who knows anything about my past life. Surely you can see that?'

'He could give us the address.'

She was surprised how insistent Ford was being. 'That's impossible. He hasn't even left me his phone number. He lives in Richmond but I don't know where. There's no alternative—I have to go with him. I'm sorry.'

Ford didn't look as though he believed her. She wanted to throw herself into his arms, tell him how much she loved him and how she regretted that he couldn't be the one to take her on this exciting journey into her past.

'But you will let me know what happens,' he asked, 'the second you get back? I've shared so much with you that I don't want to miss out on this.'

'Of course I will,' she said warmly.

'Promise?'

Kay smiled. 'I promise. I'll even ring you from Staffordshire if I discover anything of true importance.' She was hoping that everything would become clear in her mind, that every detail that was missing would slip into place. It was lot to ask, she knew, but it was what she wanted more than anything in the world. She probably wanted it even more than she wanted Ford's love— which was saying something. In her own mind he was well and truly lost to her so it was no use wishing for the impossible. But she *could* wish for her memory.

It was a further half-hour before Ford yawned and declared that he supposed he ought to be going.

'I hadn't expected you back,' she said. 'I thought you'd be staying with Karina. You're hardly being fair on her, are you?'

He frowned fiercely. 'You surprise me, Kay. Are you saying that you don't care after all that we've gone through together?'

'It's simple,' she said, desperately trying to ignore the hurt in her heart. 'You thought I was Karina. You gave me your love under a misapprehension.'

'But you fell in love with me as well.'

'I don't think so,' she answered. '*You* kept trying to tell me I was in love with you, but deep down inside I knew I wasn't. When I finally said it, it was only because I was trying to keep you happy. You were so disappointed in me. I felt I owed it to you.'

Ford's eyes narrowed as he looked at her intently for several long seconds. 'Is that the truth, Kay?'

She swallowed hard and nodded.

'I can't believe you would pretend to love me just to keep me happy. It doesn't make sense.'

'It was the only way I could repay you for all you've done,' she said quietly, unhappily, hating having to lie but finding it a necessity.

'You would have married me if Karina hadn't turned up?'

Kay nodded again.

'And what would you have done if Karina had put in an appearance *after* we were married?'

'Heavens!' she protested. 'That's an unfair question. Isn't it about time you went? Karina must be wondering what's happened to you. Incidentally, why did you come here?'

'Karina left her lipstick in the bathroom. I said it would wait until morning but, no, she had to have it now.' He sounded indulgent, as though he didn't mind at all that she had sent him out at midnight for something that wasn't of any importance.

'Besides,' he added, 'it gave me the opportunity to check up on you. I hate the thought of—'

'Will you please stop fussing?' Kay cried. 'I walked into Richmond today, for goodness' sake. I did some shopping, I had coffee—I did everything I've always done. I can easily look after myself.'

'You *walked*?' he asked incredulously. 'On your crutches?'

'No, on my hands,' she retorted scathingly. 'Actually, it was easy once I got into the rhythm of it.' She refrained from telling him how tired it had made her arms and how much energy it had taken out of her.

He heaved an unhappy sigh which came from somewhere deep in his belly. 'Did you also walk back?'

She shook her head. 'I came in a taxi with Charles.'

He was clearly unhappy about that as well, and she threw him a despairing look.

Finally he got up, went to the bathroom to retrieve the forgotten lipstick and then bent to where she still sat on the settee so that he could kiss her goodnight. 'I hate the thought of Charles kissing you,' he growled from somewhere deep in his throat. 'I hope you didn't allow it.'

His proprietorial attitude annoyed her. It was nothing to do with him any more what she did. But she was also angry with herself for allowing her senses to sharpen, to anticipate the sweetness of his kiss, and in self-defence

Kay said brittlely, 'I don't really think that it's any of your business.'

He drew back instantly, a harsh frown cleaving his brow. 'What the hell's that supposed to mean?'

'It means,' she said, her mouth firm and her eyes a brilliant, glittering blue, 'that you have Karina now. I no longer mean anything to you.'

'Oh, yes, you do,' he retorted firmly, frowning at this new Kay who was suddenly trying to distance herself from him. 'You're still very much a part of my life. You don't really think I'd wash my hands of you just like that?'

She tossed her head, her eyes still flashing. 'I wish you would. I see no point in you taking any further interest in me. I'm not who you thought I was. Surely that's excuse enough? Surely that's the end of the story?'

Ford stared at her as though she had gone out of her mind, the skin drawn tightly across his handsome face and his lips a narrow, straight line. 'Kay,' he said, his voice quiet and carefully controlled, 'I've lived with you for many long months. I know everything there is to know about you. I've developed very real feelings for you. They are not something I can throw away at the toss of a hat.'

She noticed he'd not said that he'd fallen in love with her. It was a serious omission, telling her all too clearly what the truth of the matter was. She kept her face expressionless as she answered. 'I don't expect you to. It would be nice if we remained friends, but we can no longer live in each other's pockets.'

He gave a fierce growl of disbelief, anger and pain. 'I always knew that when Charles Forester came back into your life he would cause trouble. But I—'

Kay held up her hand. 'You're forgetting, Ford, that

you thought it was Karina who'd had an affair with him. It was Karina you were angry with, not me. In fact, as I'm not the person you thought I was, I can do what I like with my life. So you getting all uptight about me being friendly with Charles doesn't make sense. You ought to be grateful I'm getting out of your hair.'

'It makes sense to me.' Flint-like dark eyes bored into her face, and his voice was hard and accusing. 'Doesn't the fact that I've devoted so much time to you mean anything? Are you really just going to close the door and forget all about me?'

Kay searched his face to see if she could see any emotion, anything at all to tell her that he still loved her, that he had feelings for her, that Karina was a part of his past but nothing at all to do with the present or the future.

There was nothing.

A veneer of hardness was painted over his face, and even his eyes were expressionless. She shivered and said quietly, 'It's the only way forward. I will always be grateful to you. It was more than I could expect any man to do. And, as I've said to you before, I intend to pay you back every penny you've spent on me.'

'Since you don't have a job I see that as an impossibility,' Ford returned cuttingly. 'Unless, of course, you become Lord Forester's mistress. Silly me, why didn't I think of that?' he snarled. 'It will be the answer to all your problems, won't it? It will get you away from me and give you financial security at the same time.'

Kay wanted to scream at him to shut up, to stop making ridiculous accusations, but for some reason her tongue cleaved to the roof of her mouth and she could say nothing.

'I wonder if he will get the same enjoyment out of

your body? I wonder if he will be as...respectful as I was where your virginity was concerned? I wonder—?'

She found her voice. 'Shut up, Ford. Stop it. What's got into you? Don't you want me to be happy? Don't you want me to trace my family? To find out who I really am? That is all Charles is going to do.'

But it was clear from Ford's stony expression that he didn't believe her, that he thought that whatever had started before her accident was going to carry on and develop into something deeper.

'I think maybe you don't know what you're letting yourself in for,' he continued bitingly. 'Charles Forester is a womaniser. You'll end up getting hurt. His offer to accompany you in your search for your family won't end there.'

Kay's chin lifted proudly. 'I think I'm capable of handling the situation,' she told him coolly. 'What's wrong with you, Ford? Why all these niggles? Why the dire warnings? You know nothing about Charles. You've nothing on which to base your pathetic insinuations or your petty accusations. If you can't be pleased for me then keep away, keep your snide comments to yourself. It might be best if you keep away from me altogether.'

She took a deep breath and tried to ignore the hammer blows of her heart, willing herself not to break down in front of him. She had to be in perfect control. She mustn't let him see by even the flicker of an eyelash that it was torturing her to say these things.

Kay was unprepared for Ford's groan of outrage and the fierce heat that blazed from his eyes. It hit her like a physical force, making her flinch and look at him with fear in her eyes.

'I'd be careful, Kaylee Philips, what you say,' he warned. 'It wouldn't be very nice, would it, to find your-

self out on the street? Or are you counting on Prince
Charming finding you some place to live? Maybe he'll
set you up in a little love-nest? Share himself between
you and his wife? Is that what you want?' he finished
sneeringly.

'You're despicable,' she spat. 'You know nothing of
my relationship with Charles. He's an honest, decent
man who's going out of his way to help me.' But not
as much as Ford had done, she thought despairingly.
Ford had given up so much for her and had given her
so much of himself that she ought not to be speaking to
him like this. She ought to be thanking him and showing
him how grateful she was instead of insisting that he
left.

His eyes grew hard, his face a granite-like mask. 'I'm
sorry it's come to this, Kay. I never expected it, never
wanted it. All I've ever wanted is your happiness. But
if you prefer someone else to provide it then I'll do the
honourable thing and bow out of your life.'

He headed towards the door and Kay wanted to call
him back. She even extended her hand towards him but
he didn't see. He didn't turn or speak again—he simply
opened the door and closed it quietly behind him.

She would have preferred him to slam it and give vent
to his anger, instead of this cool control that was destroy-
ing her. She could blame no one but herself. She had
effectively banished him. And why? Because she had
found a twin sister. What ought to have been a time for
celebration was turning into a nightmare.

'Charles, is this it?' Kay looked eagerly at her compan-
ion as they turned off the main road to drive between a
pair of handsome black and gold wrought-iron gates.

He smiled and nodded. They had been travelling for

almost three hours and she had wriggled in her seat with nervous anticipation for almost all of that time. She had refused to stop anywhere for a rest and refreshment, wanting only to reach their destination.

Thursday and Friday had been black days. She'd heard nothing from Ford and nothing from Charles either. She'd sat in the apartment and waited with only the ridiculous smiling clowns for company.

She'd spoken to them and had told them exactly what she thought of Ford for wanting to remain friends when he must have known it would crucify her. She'd also told them how deeply she loved him and that she despaired of her love ever fading away.

'Where's the cottage? Where's your house?' she wanted to know, deliberately shutting out all painful thoughts of Ford.

'The house will be coming into view at any second,' he told her. The trees had given way to open pasture where a herd of Friesians was grazing. Even as he spoke they rounded a bend and an impressive white mansion came into view. 'The cottage is on the other side. You won't see it from here.'

As they drew closer Kay waited impatiently for her memory to return. She wanted to recognise the building, the grounds, the cows, anything. *Anything!*

It was an incredible disappointment when nothing happened. Nevertheless, she clung to the hope that it was too soon. She must give herself time. Perhaps it was the cottage that would do it, not the house, and she willed Charles to drive on past it but he didn't. He drew the Porsche to a halt and helped her out, and together they went inside.

The major part of the property, he told her sadly, now belonged to the National Trust, but he had his own private rooms in the west wing and it was to these that he took her.

'I'm sure you must be thirsty and hungry,' he said, pressing a button which summoned his housekeeper. In a very short space of time breakfast arrived, which they ate at a small round table placed strategically in front of a bay window where they could look out on the grounds at the back.

There were formal gardens, and beyond them a river curved away into the distance, and more fields with more cows, but she could see no cottages. And none of it meant anything to her.

She hardly touched her bacon and egg, and merely sipped her tea, staring contemplatively through the window instead.

'The cottage is just beyond those trees,' Charles informed her.

'Can we go and see it?' Kay asked eagerly.

'As soon as we've finished. You've hardly eaten a thing. Isn't it to your liking? Shall I ask Helen to—?'

'I'm not hungry,' Kay cut in. 'It's very nice, but I want only to see the cottage to find out if—if I can remember anything.'

'Of course,' he said remorsefully. 'I should have taken you there straight away. Do forgive me. I was rather hungry myself and—'

'It's all right, Charles,' she said. 'Carry on, finish your meal.' But she was seething with impatience and the second he had put down his knife and fork she jumped to her feet. 'Shall we go?'

The cottage was built of grey stone and sheltered by a huddle of trees. A tiny, neat garden stood in front of it and a cobbled path led to a bright blue front door with a shiny brass knocker.

'Mrs Johnson is expecting us,' he said. 'I've told her all about you.'

In her excitement Kay had almost forgotten that someone else was living in the cottage, but as she stood there, waiting for the door to open, she experienced the strangest feeling. It was more a sensation than actual recognition of anything and she clenched her hands tightly in front of her, her eyes wide and expectant as a plump, motherly woman appeared in the doorway.

She had a round face and all her features seemed to be scrunched together in the middle. Her greying hair was neat and short and didn't really suit her, but she was smiling warmly and welcomingly. 'Good morning, sir. Good morning, Miss Philips. Please, do come in.'

The room they entered was the same room Kay had recalled—the same leaded windows, the same fireplace, the same shape. Only the furniture and furnishings were different. She stood in the middle of it, both Mrs Johnson and Charles Forester forgotten, and turned slowly, taking everything in.

Other than the fact that it was definitely the room where she had played with her kaleidoscope, no other memories came back. She was dreadfully disappointed. When she looked at the other two they were watching her expectantly.

She grimaced and felt tears fill her eyes. 'I recognise the room,' she said huskily and quietly, 'but that's all.'

'What did you expect?' asked Charles gently. 'That everything would rush into place? I think that's expecting too much. I think it will be a gradual progression.'

Mrs Johnson nodded, as though agreeing, but she looked sad, too. 'Spend the day here, if you like,' she said. 'Look around the other rooms. Do whatever you like. I don't mind, I really don't. I wish there was something I could do to help.'

'You don't know where my mother went?' Kay asked her.

'I'm sorry, no,' the woman replied. 'The cottage was empty when I moved in. And none of the other staff knew where your mother had gone either. She kept herself very much to herself, I'm afraid. I did a bit of enquiring after the earl phoned to tell me you were coming, but there have been staff changes since your mother left—it's been almost ten years now—and there's no one here who remembers her. Would you like a cup of tea?'

Kay shook her head, disappointment heaping on disappointment. It looked as though this was going to be a futile trip after all.

'It's must be awful for you, losing your memory,' added Mrs Johnson conversationally. 'I would hate it. And I really wish there was more I could do.'

'Can I look around?' Kay asked.

'Of course. Feel free,' the woman said at once.

While Mrs Johnson and Charles Forester sat and talked quietly, Kay limped through into the kitchen and the bathroom, then hauled herself up the stairs to the two bedrooms. All was clean and neat and smelt of furniture polish—but had absolutely no memories for her.

Kay sat on the side of the bed in the smallest of the rooms and looked out the window at the rolling green fields and thick hedgerows, at clusters of trees looking for all the world as though they were deep in conversation, at the occasional glint of water where the river wended its way into the distance. There was no other building as far as the eye could see.

As she sat there with her eyes closed and let herself drift, Kay knew for certain that this had been her room as a child. She had sat at this window a thousand times before and looked out at this very scene. She had made paper boats and sailed them in the river. Occasionally Charles had joined her.

She could see him now as a very young man, a boy just a few years older than herself. He used to cheat, throwing pebbles at her boat so that it would sink and his would win, and she used to get angry with him and flail her little fists on his chest.

She waited for more memories but nothing else came, and eventually she made her slow way back downstairs. They both looked at her expectantly.

'You used to sail paper boats with me, didn't you, Charles?'

He looked delighted. 'Yes, I did. You remember?'

'And you used to cheat, didn't you, just so that you would win?'

'I must confess,' he said with a rueful grimace, 'that, yes, I did. I couldn't let a slip of a girl beat me, could I? What else do you remember?'

It was Kay's turn to grimace. 'Nothing, except that I think I used to sleep in the smallest bedroom. But that's logical, isn't it? I would have slept there. Maybe I don't remember it.'

'You're doing well,' he said encouragingly. 'I was just saying to Mrs Johnson that perhaps I should take you on a ride around the area to see if anything triggers a chord. It might be that your mother didn't move far. Would you like that?'

Kay nodded eagerly. She was willing to do anything that might aid her recall.

They spent hours driving and nothing happened. In the end Charles said that he thought that maybe they should head back to Richmond. 'There's nothing else I can do for you,' he remarked sadly.

'I was hoping,' said Kay, 'that we could stay the night and look some more tomorrow.'

Charles shook his head. 'I'm sorry, I have to be back. We're having guests for lunch tomorrow and my wife wouldn't be very happy if I failed to turn up.'

Kay nodded. 'Of course. She didn't mind you bringing me here today?' On Wednesday he'd said his wife was in France, doing some research for a book she was writing, and Kay had somehow gained the impression that she was still there.

'Not when I explained the situation.'

'Did we ever meet? Does she know me?'

'Unfortunately not,' he said. 'I didn't meet her until long after you and your mother had left the estate. I do wish my parents were still alive, especially my mother. She used to take a keen interest in all of her employees. She might have known where you moved to.'

'You're very young for your parents to have died,' she said. 'What happened?'

A shadow crossed his face. 'My father died in a riding accident about three years ago. My mother had a heart attack when she heard about it and never recovered.'

'How awful,' said Kay. 'It must have been heartbreaking for you, losing them both together like that.'

He nodded, then deliberately changed the subject, and soon after that they were on the motorway, speeding back south.

In the days that followed Kay expected Ford to phone her, and was painfully disappointed when he didn't. Nor did Karina get in touch. Were they having such a good time that they couldn't spare her a thought? Or was Ford taking her at her word and keeping out of her life?

Whichever it was, it made her feel no better. The void she was stuck in seemed larger and blacker than ever. She was grateful to Charles for what he had done, but she hadn't arranged to see him again. There was no point when he couldn't help her any more.

She resigned herself to not ever remembering, and couldn't wait for the day when she had the plaster taken off. As soon as that happened she fully intended to get a job, even if it was a job as a shop assistant. She needed to do something—to be earning, to find somewhere else to live. She needed to get out of this apartment, which held too many memories of Ford.

The phone rang one evening just as she was getting ready for bed, and her heart lurched when she heard Ford's familiar voice. He said without preamble, 'Kay, I have some good news for you. I think I've found your mother.'

CHAPTER ELEVEN

'KAY, are you still there?'

'Yes,' she said faintly. 'I'm here. I can't believe what you've just said.' How could it be? How could Ford have found her mother?

'It's true,' he confirmed. 'Can I come over? Is it too late? Are you in bed?'

Even if she had been, it would have made no difference. She wanted him here, now, and she wanted to hear what he had to say. How had he known where to look? And why had he undertaken the task when he had other, much more important things, like Karina, to claim his attention?

Maybe it was so that he could wash his hands of her entirely—get her out of his apartment, send her back to wherever she had come from. But Kay knew that she was doing him an injustice. Ford wasn't that type of person. 'No, I'm up,' she said. 'Please come. This is incredible. How did—?'

'I'll tell you when I get there,' he said. 'I'll be just a few minutes.' And the line went dead.

They were the longest minutes Kay had ever spent. She was both excited and fearful at the same time.

It was unbelievable that he had found her mother, the one person who would be able to fill in all the blanks in her life. Totally unbelievable.

Kay expected Karina to accompany Ford to share in telling her the good news, and was surprised when he came alone. She welcomed him in and bombarded him with questions even before the door was closed.

'Hey, wait a minute,' he said, laughing. 'I can't answer them all at once.'

'So tell me how you found her, how you knew where to look? I thought you'd given up on me when I didn't hear from you.'

'I wouldn't do that, Kay, you should know me better than that,' he remarked reprovingly. 'I knew you were back. I'd cajoled one of your neighbours into ringing me the moment you returned. Then I went along to see Charles.'

'Charles?' she asked in astonishment. 'But you don't know where he lives.'

'I do now,' he said. 'I made it my business to find out. I wanted to know what had happened when you visited your old home.'

'You could have asked me,' she said, disappointment that he had chosen not to tightening her throat.

His eyebrows rose questioningly, disapprovingly. 'You could have phoned and told me.'

Kay winced. 'So why did you bother?'

'Because I care,' he answered quietly.

Because he felt sorry for her, she was sure he meant, not because he loved her! She tried to ignore the pain her heart. 'Tell me where my mother is,' she said urgently.

'She lives in a little village called Bradley near the county town of Stafford, about twenty minutes' drive from Charles Forester's place. She remarried last year to someone named Martin Paris and she's been away on a world tour ever since. She got back a couple of weeks ago.'

'So you've seen her? You've spoken to her?' Kay asked eagerly.

'No,' he answered, shaking his head. 'No, I haven't. I didn't think I should be the person to tell her what had happened to you.'

'Oh, Ford.' Kay couldn't stop her tears. They were like a spring, which had almost run dry, welling up again. When he held her, put his arms around her and drew her close, she rested her head on his shoulder as she tried to imagine what it would be like to talk to the woman she had always known as her mother.

Ford felt her trembling and his arms tightened. He stroked her hair back and rained kisses on her brow. 'I know this is the answer to your prayers, Kay. And I'm truly happy for you. I'll take you to see her whenever you wish.'

'Now?' she asked eagerly.

'It's a bit late, I think,' he said with a wry smile, 'but first thing in the morning. Or do you think you should phone first? I have her number.'

Kay thought for a moment and then shook her head. 'I'd rather go. I want to meet her face to face. How did you find her? How did you find out where she lives?'

Ford smiled. 'It was easy once I knew roughly where she lived. I put an advertisement in the local paper.'

'And my mother answered it?' Kay's blue eyes widened dramatically.

'Not exactly,' he said with a wry smile, 'but Martin did. He wanted to find out what it was all about in case it was bad news. Apparently, you never approved of him and were very much against the marriage, to the extent of arguing with your mother about him.

'Your mother thought that when she returned from her round-the-world trip you'd be back from your own travels. But there was nothing—no message, no letters, no postcards, nothing. She thinks you want nothing more to do with her. She thinks you've washed your hands of her completely.'

'Oh, Lord,' Kay said, her eyes filling with tears again. 'Maybe I *should* ring her. Put her out of her misery.'

'I don't think a few more hours will hurt,' Ford said quietly.

Kay nodded. 'You do realise, Ford, that this is something else that I'm never going to be able to thank you for. You didn't have to do this—you didn't have to go to all this trouble—and yet you have, and I'll be eternally grateful. How am I ever going to repay you?' Ford had proved yet again—if any more proof was needed—what a remarkable man he was.

'A kiss would be payment enough,' he told her quietly.

Kay's eyes opened wide as she looked up at him, her heart leaping. A kiss sounded such a little thing, a pathetic reward for all he had done, and yet the very thought of it excited her senses and set every nerve end tingling in anticipation.

She had never expected to feel his lips on hers again. She'd expected him to remain loyal to Karina. So why was he asking to kiss her? Or was she reading more into it than he'd intended? There were kisses—and there were kisses! She was thinking of the sort of kiss a man gave the woman he loved or desired, while very probably Ford was thinking of the kiss of a friend.

Closing her eyes, she lifted her mouth. Whatever he was offering she would accept gratefully. She was unprepared, however, when the kiss—which began with the merest brush of his lips on hers—developed into something much deeper, far more sensual than anything she had expected. It was not animal hunger or fierce possession, but as though he wanted to drink from her life force, gradually draining all the energy from her until her legs threatened to buckle.

'I think that's payment enough, Ford,' she said, gently pushing him away.

'If you're sure?' He raised an eyebrow quizzically. 'You're the one who's paying.'

'Of course I'm sure,' she said softly.

'In that case I'll leave you to get your sleep. What time do you want to leave?'

'The crack of dawn,' she told him, unable to help feeling disappointed that he had so willingly stopped kissing her. He'd made no attempt to prolong it, surely proving that Karina was the true love of his life. 'Karina won't mind you spending the day with me?' she asked, forcing a smile, determined to hide her chagrin.

Ford shook his head. 'Not at all. She has lots of things she wants to do, lots of friends she spends time with.'

'Did she not want to come and meet my mother? Have you told her?'

'Of course I have,' he said. 'And naturally she does want to meet her, but she thought it best for you to make this first trip alone. It will be an emotional meeting. She didn't want to spoil your moment.'

Although Kay went to bed as soon as Ford left she couldn't sleep. She was far too excited. No one could possibly understand what it was like for her to have no knowledge of her past life—no memories of school or friends or boyfriends or what she did for a living.

Tomorrow, thanks to Ford, all would be revealed. She couldn't wait.

*   *   *

As they left the M6 motorway near Stafford Kay's heart began to hammer violently and she clutched the edge of her seat. Soon now, soon…

Ford had picked her up at six that morning and it was now nearly half past nine because they had been caught in the rush-hour traffic. But they were almost there and she couldn't contain her excitement.

Having sorted out his route on a road map, Ford followed winding lanes until they reached the village of Bradley. They found the house easily, one of several new ones which had been built on the outskirts, and when Ford stopped his car he took Kay's hand and squeezed it comfortingly.

'I don't remember it,' she said quietly, looking at the red-brick, two-storied building, with its neat white net curtains at the windows and an immaculate front lawn. 'What if I don't remember my mother either? She brought me up and loved me and cared for me, and if I don't know her, then—'

'Shh, my sweet. Let's cross that bridge when we come to it.' He slid out and moved around the car to help her out and hand her the crutches.

'I'll be at your side,' he said as they walked up the path. 'There's no need to worry. Unless, of course, you'd rather meet your mother alone? I hadn't thought of that. I'm sorry if I—'

'No.' Kay stopped him quickly. 'I want you with me. I need you. You're the only one who knows what happened to me and what I've gone through. I'll need you to do all the talking.'

Ford looked disbelieving as he raised his hand to ring the doorbell. He glanced at his watch. 'It's twenty-five to ten,' he told her. 'Not as early as we'd planned.'

'You don't think they'll have gone out?' Kay asked in terror as no one answered.

'I'm sure not,' he said. 'Martin must know you wouldn't waste any time getting here.' This time he knocked on the letter box, and almost immediately the door opened.

A man of about Ford's age looked out at them—brown-haired, kind blue eyes, a good physique. Kay looked at him blankly. 'You don't recognise me?' he asked.

She shook her head. He was certainly far too young to be married to her mother so who was he and what was he doing here? Maybe she had a brother. The next moment a woman's voice came from over his shoulder. 'Darling, who is it? Is it the postman?'

Then the woman saw Kay and pushed him to one side. 'Kaylee. Kaylee. You've come back.' Tears rolled down her cheeks. 'Oh, my God. I've prayed for this moment. I never believed it would happen. I thought I was to be punished some more. Oh, Kaylee, Kaylee.'

Kay dropped her crutches and caught the other woman as she launched herself at her. She was held so tightly she could hardly breathe, and her mother's sobs of joy wracked her thin body.

'I think we should go indoors.' It was Ford who ushered them in, his hand on Kay's arm, sympathetic, encouraging, reassuring. It was then that Kay discovered that the young man was, indeed, her stepfather, and because of his age she could see why she had disapproved of her mother marrying him.

Yet as she looked at them, sitting together in the prettily decorated living room, Martin with his arm comfortingly around her mother's shoulders, Kay knew that whatever harsh thoughts she had harboured had been totally wrong. Age meant nothing—they were deeply in love.

It took a long time for Kay and Ford to tell their story, and Audrey Paris, a thin, frail-looking woman with blonde hair, constantly broke down in tears, especially when Kay told her about Karina turning up.

'And you really can't remember anything?' Audrey asked at length.

Kay shook her head, suddenly realising that she was holding Ford's hand and that he had sat by her the whole time with her hand in his, his strength her strength.

She'd hoped for a miracle today but it hadn't happened. It was a sad thought that she could still remember nothing, but did it really matter when she had this wonderful woman as a mother? A woman who loved her and cared for her very much indeed. As they came to the end of their story Kay knew there was one question she had to ask.

'Why didn't you ever tell me that I was adopted?'

Audrey's eyes widened with shock. 'Adopted? You're not adopted, Kaylee. Whatever makes you think that?'

'Because Karina said that her father—our father—told her that you were dead.'

This time Audrey winced with very real pain.

Kay went on, 'He said that he'd gone to America because he couldn't face the memories back home in England. He made out that he loved you very much.'

'The bastard,' said Audrey with deep feeling. 'I'm sorry, I shouldn't swear but I can't help it. And I can't pretend to be sorry that he's dead, not after what he did to me.'

Eventually the whole story came out. 'Your father and I,' Audrey said sadly, tearfully, 'never got on. Our marriage was doomed from the start. We argued constantly and as I'd never been very strong it soon began to take its toll on me. When you and Karina were born my health took a further downward dive.

'Your father was no use as far as bringing you two up was concerned. He preferred to spend his time in the pub, and we got divorced when you were two years old. I was granted custody and Keith was allowed access every Sunday. But one week you had a bad cold and I wouldn't let him take you. He was furious. To punish me he never brought Karina back.'

'Never?' echoed Kay in disbelief.

Audrey shook her head, more tears cascading down her cheeks. 'I've never seen her again from that day to this,' she sobbed brokenly.

'But didn't you try to find her?' Kay asked, finding it impossible to accept that her mother would have let Karina go just like that. 'Didn't you alert the police?'

'Of course I did,' said Audrey, looking astonished that Kay had even thought such a thing. 'But by the time I'd decided he wasn't coming back it was too late. He'd taken her out of the country. I guess he had it planned all along, and if you hadn't been ill he would have taken you as well. I would have lost you both.' The sobs which shook her frail body were painful to watch.

'The police in America followed his trail for a considerable time but whenever they'd nearly caught up with him he moved on to another state. Eventually they lost him altogether.'

'Why didn't you ever tell me any of this?' asked Kay,

still clutching Ford's hand, still needing his support. This was very different from what she'd expected today.

'I was too ashamed, too guilty. I felt I should have done more. I was afraid you would hate me and turn your back on me. I couldn't take the risk of losing you as well.'

'You wouldn't have lost me, Mum,' said Kay quietly and shakily. 'Even though I can't remember, I know that I loved you very much.' Ford squeezed her hand as she spoke, as though approving of what she said, but it was the truth. She did have this feeling of closeness with this tiny woman who was her mother—her real mother, her biological mother. She wanted to reassure her and comfort her, as Ford was comforting her, so she got to her feet, limped across the room and sat beside her mother.

The two women cried in each other's arms, and Martin motioned to Ford that they should go out into the kitchen for a beer.

'I never got over losing Karina,' Audrey sobbed. 'And you cried and cried for your sister when she first went. It was heartbreaking. But gradually you got over it and eventually you forgot her altogether. But I think of her all the time. Why didn't she come with you today?'

'Because she didn't know who you really were,' Kay told her sadly. 'She'll be as happy as I am when she finds out, she really will. Why didn't I approve of you marrying Martin? I know he's a bit young but he seems nice enough and you're both obviously deeply in love.'

'It was precisely that—because he was so young,' said her mother with a wry smile. 'You said it was indecent. We worked together and you'd heard rumours but you didn't believe them until I brought him home. We had the devil's own argument afterwards.

'I tried to make you understand that I'd lived for twenty-four years without a man in my life and that I deserved to be loved again. But you wouldn't have it. When Martin won some money on the lottery and we decided to get married and blow it all on a world tour you got so angry.

'I think you thought you would be pushed out, that I would transfer my love from you to Martin. That's the last thing I would ever do, my darling. I love you so very, very much.'

Kay grimaced. 'I can't believe I acted so selfishly. Was that why I decided to go and work abroad?'

'No.' Audrey shook her head. 'You'd been talking about it for a long time. It was something you'd always wanted to do. And your plans were made before ours. It was one of the reasons why I agreed with Martin's suggestion to take a twelve-month honeymoon. I didn't want to be sitting at home, worrying about you.

'I *was* worried, though, and even more so when I got back and there was no sign of you—no letters, no messages, nothing. Martin has had a lot to put up with this last few weeks. I've really tested his patience.'

'I reckon he's come through with flying colours,' said Kay. 'It's easy to see how much he loves you.'

'And it's easy to see how much Ford loves you,' her mother returned. 'Am I going to hear of an engagement soon?'

Kay shook her head vigorously. 'Ford belongs to Karina, Mum. Didn't we make that clear?'

'You did say they were engaged once, but from all I've seen today I think you are the one he really loves. Why else would he do so much for you?'

'Because he's a kind, compassionate man. He would do the same for anyone,' Kay insisted.

Her mother didn't look as though she believed her, but she said no more. When the two men entered the room, bearing crystal flutes and a bottle of champagne, Audrey said triumphantly, 'I have a splendid idea. We'll come back to London with you. I can't wait to see Karina and make my family complete.'

Kay was so quiet on the return journey that Ford asked her whether she would prefer to join her mother and Martin in the car behind. 'I know you must still have lots to talk about.'

'Yes, we do,' she agreed. There was a whole lifetime of catching up to do, a thousand and one questions she needed to have answered. 'But there'll be plenty of time for that.'

She was actually wondering whether this would be her last opportunity to spend time with Ford. In case it was, she wanted to savour these moments and add them to her chain of memories. Her mother was wrong in suspecting that Ford loved her, and very soon she would discover exactly which of her daughters it was that he favoured.

'This has been a very momentous day,' he said. 'I'm so pleased for you. You must be delirious with joy.'

'I am,' she answered fervently. 'My only regret is that I still can't remember any of my past life. Maybe the surgeon was right when he said it might never come back.'

'Does it matter now that you've found your family?' he asked, glancing across at her with a smile so warm that it melted her.

'I suppose not. I was reading a magazine article the other day about a woman who'd lost her memory ten years ago in similar circumstances, and it never returned. So if she's learned to cope then I guess I can.'

'You already are,' he told her, reaching across to put his hand over hers. 'You're a woman in a million, Kay. Don't ever think otherwise.'

If he thought that why did he seem to have transferred his affections back to Karina? she wondered unhappily, and then decided that she was being unfair. She could be a woman in a million without him being in love with her. Good Lord, he would never have spent so much time nursing her back to health if he hadn't thought she was Karina.

But she didn't move her hand from beneath his. Instead, she savoured the rush of feelings that spread through her, feelings soon to be denied her for ever. She wanted to make the most of every single opportunity, painful though they might be.

They stopped at a motorway service station for lunch, but were soon on their way again because Audrey was anxious to meet up with her other daughter, heedless of the fact that Ford had told her that Karina wouldn't be in until evening as she was visiting friends.

At Ford's massive home in Hampstead, which impressed Audrey and which she said reminded her of Charles Forester's residence, they sat and waited...and waited...and waited.

His housekeeper provided a meal, to which none of them did justice, and Kay and her mother talked nonstop. All the time she was conscious that Ford was watching her closely, causing a buzz in her veins and a quickening of her pulses.

When Karina returned it was almost midnight, and she was startled when she saw the group of people, waiting for her. And shocked beyond comprehension when she discovered that her real mother was still alive.

It was a very emotional gathering and for a while Kay almost forgot Ford. With her mother to unite them, she was finally able to accept that Karina was her twin and to feel a very strong emotional bond, and she had almost no regrets about giving Ford up to her.

When everyone began to yawn surreptitiously Ford suggested they went to bed and continued their conversation the next morning. He had already arranged with his housekeeper for Audrey and Martin to stay the night. 'And I think you should, too,' he said to Kay, his dark eyes gentle.

'Of course,' said Karina. 'You can borrow one of my nightdresses, and a dressing-gown if you wish. I have plenty with me.'

Ford helped Kay upstairs and made sure she had everything she needed. She was hoping he would kiss her before he left, but he didn't. He simply gave her a long, lingering look, which sent her blood racing, and then quietly closed the door behind him.

She had no idea what thoughts were going through his mind, whether he guessed at the torment in her soul and whether he ever wondered how she felt, after discovering that she was a twin—and not the one he loved! Or had she done such a good job of convincing him that she'd never truly loved him that he didn't lose a moment's sleep over her?

Although Kay had slept very little the previous night and ought to have slept well now, she was still wide awake over an hour after going to bed. She was very conscious that Ford was somewhere near, very possibly sharing his bed with Karina, and over and over in her mind's eye she saw him making love to her twin, saw Karina uninhibitedly responding. She found herself listening for sounds of them making love.

In the end, angry with herself, she got out of bed and belted Karina's dressing-gown around her. She made her way slowly downstairs, scorning her crutches, and went as quietly as she could to the kitchen to make herself a milky drink.

Ovaltine, she thought. It was what she had always liked as a child. She pulled herself up short. Another memory. Another piece in the jigsaw. Perhaps this was how it was going to be. Little by little everything would piece itself into a whole.

She actually smiled now as the milk in the saucepan warmed and she poured it into a china mug. Suddenly, and without warning, she heard Ford's voice close to her ear, felt his arms snake around her waist and hold her firm against him.

'What is this? Can't you sleep, my sweet one?'

'Heavens, Ford, you frightened the life out of me,' she exclaimed. He had been as quiet as the proverbial church mouse, but it was no timid mouse who held her— it was a strong, virile man with the power to shred her emotionally and melt every bone in her body.

'I wondered who it was, creeping around at this time of night—or should I say morning?' His lips nuzzled her neck, adding to the frenzy of feelings that were running out of control.

'Couldn't you sleep either?' she asked, wanting to

move away from him but finding herself immobilised. Every joint was locked, every impulse stunned.

'I haven't been to bed,' he informed her, with a further flurry of kisses that threatened her sanity. 'I've been in my study, writing letters. Actually, I'd much rather have been in bed with you, my sweet. I was just thinking about it when—'

It was at this point that Kay realised he had mistaken her for Karina. Without her crutches, and with her sister's dressing-gown almost sweeping the floor, he had made a simple mistake.

'I don't really think you ought to be doing this,' she protested weakly, even as a further tide of sensation washed over her.

'Give me one good reason why,' he growled.

If she was honest with herself Kay didn't want him to stop. She wanted to take everything he offered, whether he thought she was Karina or not. 'Someone might see us,' she demurred faintly.

'Like who?' he asked with a laugh. 'I'm willing to bet everyone's crashed out.' Very gently he turned her to face him, tilted her chin with a firm finger and brought his mouth down on hers.

A noise seemed to rush through Kay's head, building up and building up like the pressure in a volcano until it felt ready to explode. Her body was on fire, every nerve and sinew zinging with life. She couldn't push him away now, couldn't deny herself this tormenting pleasure.

He locked her hard against him and his kisses, which began very gently, soon gave way to a fierce, devouring hunger. 'Oh, my sweet one,' he murmured against her mouth. 'How much I want you. How much I love you.'

Kay felt ashamed of the way she was exploiting him, but she couldn't stop the torrent raging through her veins, or her arms from snaking around him, or her hips from pressing into his hard male body, feeling the encompassing heat that set him on fire too.

Briefly she prayed he wouldn't be angry when he found out, but only briefly for the next second she was lost in a world of sensation where nothing mattered except this man who was engulfing her.

CHAPTER TWELVE

'IT'S been a long, difficult day,' Ford murmured. 'I thought constantly of holding you like this, feeling your soft, exciting body close to mine, making endless love to you.'

Kay wished he hadn't spoken, hadn't said the words which she knew had been meant for Karina. She wanted to savour this moment. She didn't want it spoilt by reminders that he would have preferred to spend the day with her sister, instead of carting Kay halfway across the country to find her mother.

She didn't realise that her body had stiffened until he lifted his head and looked with a faint enquiring frown into her eyes. 'What's wrong, my sweet?'

It's wrong that I'm not who you think I am, she said silently. It's wrong that I should entertain such feelings for the man who's going to marry my sister. It's wrong that I didn't stop you straight away.

What her answer would have been Kay didn't know, but a sudden sound from the doorway caused them both to turn their heads. 'Oops, I'm sorry,' said Audrey, her hand over her mouth. 'I didn't realise I would be interrupting anything. I couldn't sleep and thought I'd get myself a drink.'

'The same here,' said Kay. 'Come and join me. Ford was just going.'

She felt his start of surprise. 'Please,' she whispered.

'I'd like some time alone with my mother.' It was the perfect excuse.

He nodded his understanding but even so he looked reluctant as he cupped her face between his hands and gave her one last lingering kiss.

'It makes me truly happy, Kaylee, to see you and Ford so much in love,' said Audrey as she joined her daughter by the stove.

Kay wondered how she knew which daughter she was talking to. If her mother had spotted the difference, had Ford also? It was a startling thought but one she dismissed straight away. It was natural that her mother would know—it would be instinct. Ford would have no idea. He'd already said more than once that if it hadn't been for the plaster cast he wouldn't have been able to tell them apart.

Her mother warmed more milk and they sat and drank their Ovaltine and talked over the events of the day. Then Kay asked her mother why she disliked yellow roses.

Audrey laughed. 'It's because you once cut all my prize blooms to give me as a birthday present. Instead of being pleased, I shouted at you as I'd wanted to enter them into the local flower show. You hated any yellow flowers after that. Why do you ask?'

Kay was saved from answering when, to their surprise and delight, Karina joined them, unable to sleep either, and it ended up as a real family party.

In the conversation that followed Kay discovered that she had trained as a graphic designer, exactly as her sister had, and the more they talked the more similarities in their life-style and their habits came to light. It was a strange and yet wonderful feeling. 'We must never let anyone part us again,' said Karina firmly.

'My sentiments entirely,' declared their mother.

'But I thought you were going back to America?' Kay queried with a frown.

'I was, but I've changed my mind,' announced Karina with a satisfied smile.

It took no guessing why, thought Kay bitterly. Ford's work was here. This was where he had to stay, and so Karina would stay too.

Audrey looked delighted but it was small comfort as far as Kay was concerned. It was obvious that Ford was still the big issue, the big draw, even though Karina wasn't admitting it. Any day now Kay expected their wedding plans to be announced.

Dawn had broken by the time they all went back to bed. Kay didn't even bother to get into hers. She washed and dressed and sat in a chair where she could look out of the window.

It was a beautiful clear day in early autumn. Some of the leaves on the trees had started to turn but not many. A squirrel scampered across the lawn and disappeared into the shrubbery, and a blackbird dug for worms.

Kay watched these things without really seeing them. She could think of nothing but Ford and how painful her future would be when he was married to her sister.

She was surprised when the man she was thinking about entered her room, bearing a tray with two cups and saucers and a pot of tea. Her heart began its familiar stampede of excitement. He was dressed in a pair of casual cotton trousers and a blue polo shirt. His hair was still damp from the shower, and he smelled of sandalwood and musk.

He looked surprised to see that she was up and dressed herself. 'I thought you'd still be in bed,' he said.

Kay shook her head. 'I couldn't sleep.'

'I don't think anyone slept very well last night,' he commented as he began to pour the tea.

'Why have you brought two cups?' She loved the thought of him joining her, but wasn't sure her sister would be very happy about it. 'Won't Karina be expecting you to take your tea with her?'

He smiled indulgently. 'Karina is fast asleep. I don't expect she'll wake up until lunchtime. She didn't sleep well either last night. I don't think any of us did except perhaps Martin. He's in the kitchen, drinking coffee. He says your mother is dead to the world.'

'So why did you bring tea up to me if you thought I'd be asleep as well?'

He pursed his lips in a grimace. 'It was a gamble, I guess. Aren't I wanted? Would you rather I left you to drink your tea alone?'

'No, of course not,' said Kay quickly, perhaps too quickly because he smiled his pleasure as he passed her cup to her.

'You must be very happy,' he said, 'to have your family complete.'

She nodded. 'But it's my mother I'm happiest for. She's the one who lost the most. My memory is nothing compared to what happened to her. She wants me to go and live back at home.'

Ford stilled. 'And are you going to?' he asked, looking at her as though her answer was of vital importance.

Kay nodded. 'In the short term. I shall find myself a job and eventually a flat somewhere near them. As far away from you as possible,' she added under her breath.

It was the only way she would ever be able to control her love, control the feelings that even at this moment were running rampant through every inch of her body.

She would have liked nothing more than for Ford to take her in his arms and kiss her as he had kissed her a few hours ago. But this time she wanted him to kiss her because she was Kay and because he loved her—not because she was Karina.

'Is that really what you want to do?' he asked.

'It's what I must do.'

'That wasn't my question,' he pointed out.

Kay gave a deep sigh. 'There's nothing for me here. When you're married to Karina I—'

'Who says I'm marrying Karina?' he interjected sharply with a frown.

'It's obvious,' she said. And painful. And distressing. And she didn't really want to talk about it.

'Obvious to whom? It's certainly not obvious to me.'

Kay frowned. 'But I thought—I assumed—that you would get back together. You treated me the way you did because you thought I was my sister so it was obvious that when she turned up you'd transfer your affections back to her.'

'Your eyes are blinkered, Kay. I don't think I ever really and truly loved Karina. Not the way I love you.'

'But...' Kay knew she must be hearing things. It didn't make sense. He couldn't be saying this.

'But nothing, my sweet one. It's the truth. Did you not hear me this morning when I told you that very same thing?'

Kay frowned. 'But you thought I was Karina then. I know it was wrong of me not to—'

'Kay,' he said in a very firm voice, 'I didn't think you were Karina. I knew it was you.'

'You did?' she asked in a hushed voice, her mind a whirl of confusion and hope. 'How?'

'Your response to me. Your body gives you away every time. Even now, when I'm not touching you, I can see in your eyes that you're affected by me. You can deny your love all you like, but I shall never believe it. I know you're trying to do the honourable thing but, believe me, my sweet, it's all in vain.

'Karina doesn't love me—she merely enjoyed sex with me. If I'm honest, it was the same for me, too, although I wasn't aware of it at the time. We talked about it the other day. It was one of the reasons she sought me out—to see if there were any feelings left. There were none on either side. She's found herself a new man in America—didn't she tell you that?'

Kay shook her head. 'No, she didn't tell me, and you're wrong.' She wanted to believe him. So badly she wanted to believe him. 'Because Karina says that she's not going back to America. She's going to live here in London. With you.'

'She actually said that?' he asked with a frown.

'Well—not that she was actually going to move in with you permanently but, yes, she is going to make her home here.'

He gave a stern frown. 'And you assumed it was for my sake? I think you do too much assuming, Kay.'

'Do you know differently, then?' she asked bluntly.

'Of course I do. Karina's boyfriend is moving here with his job. They are setting up home together. She's been house-hunting while she's been here, and has had all her friends looking out for houses. Hasn't she told you any of this?'

'No,' Kay said in surprise. 'I suppose I've not really seen much of her. I thought she was spending all her time with you.'

'Then you thought wrong,' Ford told her firmly. 'But I'm not here to discuss your sister. It's us I want to talk about. You said you had never loved me, Kay. You hurt me deeply. Would you care to tell me the truth now?'

Kay looked down at her cup and saucer. 'I was afraid of humiliating myself,' she said quietly, so quietly that he had to strain to hear her soft words. 'But it's true. Yes, I—I do love you. I love you very much.'

She heard his indrawn breath of deep satisfaction. 'Look at me, Kay.'

Shyly she raised her head and what she saw in his eyes sent the blood zinging through her veins. There was so much love there it quite took her breath away.

Gently he replaced her cup on the tray, together with his own, and then he helped her up from the chair and gathered her into his arms. 'My precious darling. My sweet Kay. My own true love. This is the culmination of all my dreams, you do know that?'

'For me too,' she said in a hushed voice, feeling him trembling against her, aware of her own tremors which were shaking her limbs like the leaves on an aspen tree. Her future looked suddenly bright, more so than she had ever imagined.

When he lowered his mouth over hers, his kiss told her far more than any words could have how deep his feelings for her were. Kay felt as though she had just walked over a rainbow and found the pot of gold at the end.

'Kay, my sweet one,' Ford murmured against her mouth. 'I love you so much. I will always love you. Make no mistake about that.'

'I don't really see how there is any difference between me and Karina,' she said, still suffering pangs of doubt.

He smiled and shook his head. 'Then you're blind, my angel. It's only on the surface that you're alike.'

'But I've discovered lots and lots of ways in which we are very much the same,' she told him.

'That's as may be. But where sensuality is concerned, where the emotions are concerned, where making love is concerned, there is a whole world of difference. Karina is a very dominant lover—and I'll think you'll find she is dominant in other ways, too. Whereas you, my sweet, are far more gentle and submissive.'

'And that's what you prefer—submissiveness?'

'Hell, no, Kay, don't get me wrong. When you're aroused you're a wildcat. You're all I want in a woman. Perhaps I should prove it.'

He lifted her in his arms as easily as if she'd been a child and set her down on the bed, where he proceeded to remove her clothes, feasting adoring, hungry eyes on her as he did so.

By the time he had finished Kay was burning with desire. She wanted to undress him but he wouldn't let her. He ripped his clothes off impatiently, leaving them on the floor where he stood, and then lay on the bed beside her.

What happened next was a blur. Kay was aware of nothing but the feel of Ford touching her, exciting her, arousing her. Only senses mattered—taste, smell, touch. It was exquisite, and their final coming together took her out of this world.

'Kay.'

She smiled drowsily. 'Yes?' She was lying with her back curled against him. His arm was around her, his fingers playing with her hair. They were both heavily drugged with emotion and knew it would take a very long time for the aftermath of their love-making to wear off. Kay didn't want this feeling of togetherness, of supreme happiness, of her body glowing and feeling lighter than air, to ever go.

'Will you marry me?'

She smiled to herself and said quietly, 'My mother knew.'

'Knew what?'

Kay could almost see him frowning. 'That you loved me. She said she could see it.'

'Then your mother's a very astute woman.' He nibbled her ear and teased one nipple with his fingers.

Kay sighed as a fresh surge of desire soared through her, and as she moved against him she felt him surge back into life.

'Make love to me again,' she said softly.

His fingers continued to tease and torment her, to drive her almost crazy. 'Only if you promise to marry me, my own sweet darling,' he said hoarsely.

'I promise, I promise.' Kay couldn't keep still. When Ford entered her, when she arched her body to meet him, when they became one, she knew that her happiness was complete. It didn't matter now whether she ever recovered her memory. What mattered was that this man loved her and she loved him. And together they would conquer the world.

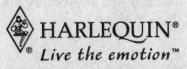

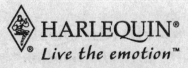

introduces an exciting new family saga with

DYNASTIES: THE DANFORTHS

A family of prominence...
tested by scandal, sustained by passion!

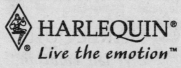

The world's bestselling romance series.

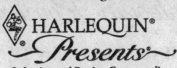

HARLEQUIN®
Presents

Seduction and Passion Guaranteed!

Back by popular demand...

She's sexy, successful and PREGNANT!

Share the surprises, emotions, drama and suspense as our parents-to-be come to terms with the prospect of bringing a new life into the world. All will discover that the business of making babies brings with it the most special love of all....

Our next arrivals will be

CONSTANTINO'S PREGNANT BRIDE
by Catherine Spencer
On sale October, #2423

THEIR SECRET BABY
by Kate Walker
On sale November, #2432

HIS PREGNANCY ULTIMATUM
by Helen Bianchin
On sale December, #2433

Pick up a Harlequin Presents® novel and you will enter a world of spine-tingling passion and provocative, tantalizing romance!

Available wherever Harlequin books are sold.

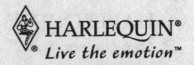

HARLEQUIN®
Live the emotion™

www.eHarlequin.com

HPEXPOD